The Sin Giver

Sam Sedou

Copyright © 2018 Sam Sedou
All rights reserved

Contents

City Gent	4
Change of Luck	13
Blast from the Past	24
Superbia	37
Gula	48
Ira	61
Reasons and Motives	77
The Show Must Go On	92
It Wasn't Personal	104
Acedia	119
Luxuria	137
Invidia	153
Avaritia	165

1 City gent

An early November evening in London's square mile. That time of year when the retailers are trying to convince us Christmas is just round the corner. It hit minus four centigrade two nights running and it was getting harder to find a place to sleep where he wouldn't be moved on by the police, or hadn't already been taken by another homeless.

He was too close to the money area to find a quiet spot where he could bed down for the night. It was his own fault for not bedding down earlier, but he needed to beg for longer to get booze money to help dull the pain that had been growing in his belly for the last week. He had thought about going to the hospital yesterday, but knew they would only tell him to eat a proper meal and try to get into a shelter for a few days. The shelters were always full; too many homeless sleeping rough these days. He knew he'd be better off if he moved North or South towards more residential areas instead of spending most of his time frequenting the City area. Deep down he knew that his fall from grace and the speed at which it happened shocked him so much that his mind needed to hold on to some vestige of his previous life; even if it's just being in the vicinity of where he used to work. He decides to walk to a road called Lexington Street, just on the edge of the business area where the transition from business to residential was apparent. He'd had luck there before where he'd found a sheltered doorway with no lighting.

David Todd shuffles the twenty minute walk in twice the time. He finally turns into Lexington Street and proceeds to find accommodation for the night. The road is lined on both sides with terraced Georgian style town houses. Most of the houses had been converted into flats, starting with the basements and rising to the third floor.

He stumbles as he takes a swig from his can of Special Brew; he had bought six cans for £4. That would last him the night and maybe have one left for breakfast if he fell asleep quickly enough. The wind is bitingly cold; effortlessly slicing through the shabby collection of old clothes stuffed with crumpled up newspaper like knives made of ice. A fleeting memory of better times in his life warms him slightly. He shrugs off the thought before any remorse can set in and sips at his dinner again. He stumbles again, this time falling to the pavement.

David a 44 year old Dorset born law graduate from Cambridge University was born to work in the City. Four years ago he took a tumble from a very successful career in the City of London as a specialist in Mergers and Acquisitions for a leading Investment Bank. White, male, English through and through, five feet nine, about twelve stones, at least the last time he stepped on a scale. His ability to spot the advantage in any scenario involving a potential takeover or merger and his uncanny knack of focusing in on the most profitable part of the deal was invaluable to any of the banks he had worked for in the past. Average looking in a bank manager kind of way, a slightly weak chin, but piercing blue eyes which seemed to read your mind as he asked questions of the company he was about to prepare a report on. He then had a full head of brown hair, but now fields a full head of grey hair, accompanied by a grey beard, which was trimmed slightly every eight or so weeks by a friendly local barber. He had lost a lot of weight over the years; maybe down to about ten stones now.

Four years ago he had it all, great job, company that lavished him with money, cars and all the corporate benefits that you would expect for a man who made them over £500 million a year in those lean times. The homeless man who now shuffles along the street once commanded teams of bank employees. His every word was obeyed. His entire focus was on making the company ever more profitable, often to the exclusion of all else, especially his family. He had a family once, a wife and two children. Mary, his wife, was three years younger than him. Blonde and attractive; not stunning, but he loved everything about her. Her smile, laugh even her angry face. Five feet six and in good shape for a mother of two she came from a strict Jewish family who did not approve of David at first, but over the years they came to accept him and gave their blessings for their daughter to marry him. They met at a Company social and hit it off immediately. The children, Ian and Vincent, were 8 and 6 the last time David saw them. Ian was a lanky, thin boy with his mother's blonde hair. Vincent was a dizzy, shy little thing who always seemed a little unfocused. David was starting to forget things about his family. Each day was a struggle to remember certain birthdays or anniversaries. Was it Ian or Vincent who has blonde hair? Memories of family days out, which were far and few between; the job was more important. David struggles to recollect any days out to a museum or gallery or the even the cinema.

As he gets to his knees he glimpses a basement window at the bottom of a stairwell to his left. The window is boarded up from the outside. He can only hope that if he removes the boards there will be no one inside and he might find a place to stay out of the open for at least one night. He struggles to his feet, the pain now dulled by the hope of a dry sanctuary. He descends the stairs to the base of the stairwell slowly careful not to alert anyone who may be living there. The top of the window is at his head height. The boards run vertically and are fixed with screws to the frame. He grabs a board receding above the cill and gives it a sharp tug not expecting it to give way. The board comes away easily bringing a smile to David's face. He continues with the other boards and they come away easily too.

It's dark in the basement; he peers in through the window to make sure there is no one living there; no sound or light. Judging by how easily the screws came away the boarding must have been there for quite some time. David climbs through the window left leg first. He half expects to hear a scream followed by someone stabbing him repeatedly with a bread knife. That would be a fitting end for him. Nope, no manic screams and the only stabbing pain was the one he already had.

He reaches into his left side coat pocket and pulls out a small box of matches. He'd learnt that even though he didn't smoke, always pick up discarded matches. He lights one and surveys the room. It's a bedroom with just a single bed in the corner. The mattress is bare and filthy. No other furnishings. Whoever left this place was gone for now not likely to return soon. He can't believe his luck. There is an ashtray on the floor next to the bed. He removes some paper from under his coat and places it in the ashtray: he lights the paper. He goes to the window and gathers the wood he had pushed through into the room. He replaces the wood carefully to make the widow looks boarded from the inside. If he could find this place others could also. Finally his luck is changing and he doesn't want to share his new cosy basement with any addicts or other hapless degenerates.

He does the best he can for now, but would make it more secure tomorrow when he has a chance to beg a few items from the construction site he passed on the way. There is a light switch by the bedroom door. As the paper burns out he approaches the door and turns the knob. The door opens and he gently pulls it towards him making sure he is truly alone. A dark passage way, he lights another match. The corridor leads to the front door of the flat. Lighting match after match he explores the small kitchen and reception area, and wow, a bathroom with a toilet. The last time he took a shit on a toilet was over two months ago. There is a white cast iron bathtub in the corner; the toilet is at the base of the tub and there is a sink against the wall opposite the toilet and tub. David reaches out and pushes the flush lever down. It flushes.

"I'm definitely going to be using that tonight" he thinks. Returning to the bedroom he flicks the light switch down not expecting anything to happen,

"Holy shit"

The light comes on. It's dim, but fucking hell, there is electricity. He struggles to comprehend what this means. Maybe someone is coming back soon and his cosy greater London pad will be gone as quickly as it came. Then he remembers that little shithole bedsit he was put in when Westminster police found him passed out and gagging on his own vomit a year after he went walkabout. It had a pay as you go electric meter. He rushes to the kitchen and opens the large cupboard to the right as he enters. There it is; a pay by coin operated electric meter. It still has £12.35 on it. That could last him a month if he was careful. He goes back to the bedroom and examines the mattress on the pine framed bed. Looks like whoever slept in the bed last didn't much like going to the toilet for a piss. He takes the mattress and uses it to block the window so no one can see the light.

Sitting on the wooden slats of the bed base David looks around him. An empty room with wooden floors, no mirrors, no wardrobes, just the single pendant light in the middle of the ceiling. He sips at his dinner still taking in his surroundings. He empathises with the room, left empty, and pissed on repeatedly. A wave of self pity washes over him and he takes another gulp.

As the brew takes effect he mulls over the events of four years ago, still desperate to understand how the fuck it had all fallen apart so quickly. He was one of the top City Executives in his field working with one of the top Investment Banks alongside six of the best professionals in their respective fields. As he tries to focus through the alcoholic haze, his belly reminds him why he might have been shitting blood lately. He doubles over still sat on the bed base. The wave of pain passes after about 5 minutes. This time it was far worse. He realises he has fallen to the floor. He pushes himself up and sits on the base.

"Christ" he thinks to himself "that felt like something was wriggling around inside me; clawing at me".

He reaches down and grabs another can of main course, clicks it open and takes a good long swig.

Over the past four years he had a lot of time to think, a lot of theories had come and gone, but there was one which seemed improbable yet the more he thought about it the more he could conceive how it could have brought about the devastation in his life. He shakes his head and says to himself.

"It can't be; that would mean the six people I trusted most would have conspired against me". David stares at the floor running the scenario in his head over and over again.

He lifts his head, his eyes open and tearing up as he has a penny drop moment.

"They did it" he speaks with a croaking voice "they worked together to fuck me over", his voice is now stronger with anger building up. "The six people who I trusted and built up from nothing did this to me" he realises he might be heard by someone in the flat above.

He stops speaking and just re-runs the scenario in his head over and over again getting angrier each time. The angrier he gets the more the pain in his stomach gets. He is about to shout in rage when the pain takes hold of him and he feels the urgent need to take a shit. He runs to the toilet loosening his trousers en-route. He plunges his behind onto the toilet seat and gives a push. Mixed emotions, anger, disappointment and hatred still welling up in him; worry about what is wrong with his stomach tempering his rage. He feels his lower intestine being grabbed, but knows this is not possible. Yet there is that wriggling and grabbing again. Maybe a tape worm he rationalises, then a huge blast of pain as something seemingly to be too big is nevertheless creeping out of his arse. He looks down between his legs, pushing his dick to one side and would have shit himself if not for the small oblong shaped lump of grey thing already coming out of him. It is covered in streaks of blood. He pushes, the anger now chased away by the fear. Maybe it's the booze and I'm asleep dreaming this. More pain, no, not dreaming, he sees what looks like a face on the lump. Two small holes where the nose should be and a slit of a mouth. No fucking eyes. He screams "No!" David shouts, not caring who hears him.

"Oh fuck! Oh fuck! What the hell!" he wants to grab it and pull it out of him.

Another blast of pain, his body now trembling uncontrollably, he cannot resist looking. He doesn't want to but he is as mesmerised as he is revolted by what's happening. He struggles to look between his legs to see this thing coming out of his anus. The thing is wriggling from side to side trying to extricate itself from his arse. David shouts in agony.

"Fuck no! Fuck no!" He pushes hard just wanting it out.

The lump slides out further. It has arms. Two short little arms with three fingers or what looks like fingers on each arm. Then a sudden rush through his arse as the rest of the lump passes, almost effortlessly, and lands in the toilet. He springs up and whirls around to look at the thing he had just shit out. He half expects to see an umbilical cord attached, but no thank god. His arse is hurting bad, but he has to see this thing. There in the water face up using the little arms to try to get up above the water level. David's mind races with all kinds of thoughts. This can't be happening. How can this thing have been living in him all this time?

"Jesus, what's happening to me?" He is scared.

As he watches the creature he shouts "Drown you fucker."

He looks at it with a weird fascination as the thing keeps going down and coming up clawing at the pan of the toilet. He suddenly thinks "What if I have more of this thing in me?"

He looks around and finds an old cleaning cloth on the floor. Picking up the cloth he carefully reaches down into the toilet and picks up the creature. He tosses it into the sink and runs the tap to wash his hand.

"No soap, fuck, no soap" like that was his main worry.

As David stares at the thing borne of him he feels no more pain. In fact the pain is gone and a strange sense of well being comes over him. He still has a dull ache in his arse where the thing forced its way out. Could this be some sort of mutant tape worm? As he bends over to take a closer look he contemplates whether there may have been some damage to his rectum. How would he explain this to the A&E nurse? The lump is shaped like one of those Russian dolls, but all grey, with two holes for a nose and a slit, no lips, just a slit for a mouth and no eyes.

"What the fuck have you been feeding on?" As he peers closer he is surprised. "It's fucking breathing", he steadies himself and moves closer. About a foot away from it he sniffs the air "doesn't smell like shit", he moves in closer and then he hears it hiss something. The slit of a mouth opens exposing upper and lower lines of tiny sharp cannibal like teeth. As its mouth opens and closes it hisses what sounds like the word "Kiss", David moves in closer his face now just inches from the thing's mouth. He listens, sounds like "Kiss", he thinks to himself "surely not the kiss of life?" Then he hears the words properly.

The lump hisses out the words "Kill six", David recoils in disbelief.

How could it know what he was thinking? For a moment before the ordeal of passing this thing out he was thinking of how he would mutilate those six back stabbing scum of the earth ex-colleagues. Surely this is just a coincidence? He leans in to listen again and again.

The lump raises its arms and hisses repeatedly "Kill six".

2 Change of Luck

David washes and wraps it in newspaper then rests it on the bed base. He stands up and stares at it. His mind wrestling with the possibilities of what it could be. He had slept in some filthy rat infested places and eaten and drunk some dirty stuff in the past four years. He'd seen some weird shit, some real, some probably not, but a talking, mind reading creature which came out of his arse? That was well fucking new.

"Maybe its worth something in the scientific community" he thinks for a second then discards the idea just as quickly "wouldn't want to see that process documented."

David finishes the can of larger. His arse was feeling much better now, but the mental images would take a lot of Special Brew to eliminate. As he peels open another tin the creature moves its arms; David sips the lager then moves closer to the lump. The lump is now fairly animated for a creature with only two movable appendages. Its mouth opens and closes quickly.

"Can't be" David thinks "It's thirsty?"

David slowly uprights the lump like a patient being raised to take a sip of water. He pours a small amount of lager into the slit of a mouth being careful not to let the tin touch the creature for fear of contamination. The lump laps at the liquid, its surprisingly long tongue moving in and out swiftly taking in all that is poured.

"Definitely mine" he says out loud then feels a shiver go down his spine.

Whatever this is he was no longer afraid of it. What the hell could it do to him? He would wait till morning then go to the hospital with the lump and try to explain what happened without everyone pissing themselves with laughter. He rests the lump down and gets ready to sleep. As he lies on the floor he realises the stomach pain is gone completely replaced by a feeling he hadn't felt for a while. He feels hungry.

"Some food would be good; maybe tomorrow." David falls asleep.

A banging noise pulls David out of a bad dream about a giant worm.

"What the hell?" David's eyes open.

There's someone at the front door. He wonders if last night was just a dream; then he sees it. The creature is on the floor. He gets up and moves to answer the door with some trepidation. Was he about to be chucked out?

Through the letterbox David enquires "Who is it?"

"Your delivery Sir" comes back the answer.

Intrigued David opens the door to a young man about twenty years old dressed in a yellow jump suit with Sunshine Diner written across the chest in red "Your order Sir?" the young man holds out a bag.

"I didn't order anything. Don't even have a phone".

The young man shakes his head realising they've been pranked again "Bloody Uni kids. Same stupid prank every year. Listen fella, you can have the food for half price if you want."

"I'd like to, but if you take a closer look you may suspect I don't even have money for the electricity meter."

David begins to close the door just to get that delicious smell of a cooked breakfast away from his groaning belly. The young man stops the door "Listen man, we're only going to have to chuck the food so you may as well have it. No charge."

He hands the bag to David who accepts it with his thanks. The young man dashes off to his next, hopefully genuine delivery.

David moves to the bedroom eager to see what delights are in the bag. A full English for two including toast, hash browns and two cups of coffee. He grabs the plastic cutlery and sets about the free meal. As he eats, his new friend stirs and moves its mouth quickly. David picks up some scrambled eggs about to feed the lump. He ponders his own sanity as he is about to feed the creature. He had read somewhere that many homeless people create a "friend" to fill the void of loneliness. Some were just fucking nuts. If this was just in his mind why create such an odd disgusting thing? And why have it come out of his arse? He feeds the creature by holding bits of the food over its mouth and letting them fall into the slit. The creature guzzles the food down its fat, neck less form.

David wonders "Maybe I can get some money for it; a talking mutant tape worm, got to be worth something" he then immediately dismisses the idea. It has been over four years since he last saw his wife and kids, the last thing he wanted them to see was good old dad on TV famed for shitting out a mutant worm.

Besides, since shithead "Hmm, that's what I'm going to call you, Shithead," came along his luck has changed. He is in a room with electricity and water, eating a free breakfast delivered to his door. He had finally figured out who had fucked him over and how; now if he could get cleaned up he could get close to one of them to get some answers.

Shithead wriggles and hisses "Kill six."

David stares at this thing spitting out words that resonate with the feelings of hatred he has for these people. The words excite him. The thought of killing them makes his heart race lifting his spirit.

"But how?" He asks Shithead.

The six who betrayed him are Roger Caldwell and his wife Iris, Deepak Patel, Michael Howard, Susan Chang and David's best friend Danny Havers. Roger and Iris were corporate lawyers, Deepak a lobbyist, Michael and Susan corporate finance specialists and Danny was David's right hand, helping in the management of the various projects. David had trusted Danny completely.

Roger was an extremely overweight forty eight year old American who had come to the UK from New England to study Law at Cambridge University.

A bright nineteen year old his parents were eager to get him away from rumours that he had banged up the maid. His parents had money and contacts which made it easy to facilitate an abortion and to assist with Cambridge's expansion costs subject to their son being afforded a place at the University.

Iris was fifteen years younger than Roger and met him while being interviewed for a position at Roger's law firm. He was besotted immediately with the young brunette. It didn't matter what her CV said or how the interview went, he wanted her. Her smooth, pale skin and that body, he just had to have her. Iris knew she had him and played with him for six months before she let him fuck her. He proposed the same night and had been married eight years the last time David saw them.

There were lots of whispers that Iris was fucking around with the male trainees at the firm, but Roger never seemed to know, and if he did then he turned a blind eye. Their marriage was on autopilot. Roger seemed to drift in and out of bouts of depression over the years. When he was depressed he turned to food. Roger was a little on the podgy side when he met Iris, but over the years had ballooned up to a morbidly obese twenty two stones.

Deepak, son of East African immigrants, he studied politics at Central London University. At thirty six he had forged a reputation for being an extremely effective lobbyist and a deal maker for big business and government groups. Slim built, five six, but what he lacked in height he made up for with his mouth.

A liking for designer wear and the finer things in life he always had to look the part. His impeccable taste extended to all aspects of his life. Clothes, cars, Central London apartment and the accompanying designer furnishings. He resisted his parent's insistence to marry a nice Guajarati girl; mostly because he is gay; a fact not hidden from his family, friends and colleagues. His parents chose not to believe it. You know, a passing phase.

Michael was a quiet careful man. The type who preferred to listen to everything first before speaking. Forty two years old, six feet two, slim build. He looked closer to fifty five with the demeanour of a man carrying the all the world's problems on his shoulders. Also a Cambridge graduate, he specialised in Corporate Finance. Single; his only surviving family, dear old mum, who he had enrolled into a care home due to advanced dementia.

Susan, an unusual woman in that despite her high intellect and razor sharp reasoning skills, she made it a habit to avoid confrontation. This is probably why she enjoyed the company of accounts and numbers so much. After all the numbers never lie and she was always able to tell if someone was trying to make them lie.

Numbers were something she could rely on always. Half Chinese, half Irish, Susan took her mum's blonde hair. Five feet two she always dressed modestly. Under the modest clothing were the signs of a very sexy physique. A pretty girl with dimples on her cheeks she looked ten years younger than her thirty four.

Soon after joining David's team she hooked up with Danny, falling for his banter and the two have been together since.

Danny, once his best friend and best man at David's wedding; now the scum who must have put it all together. An inch taller than David's five nine, good looking in a clean cut, chiselled jaw kind of way. Danny hit the gym every morning and was an avid dieter. He was in great shape for his age and it was easy to see why women were drawn to him. Same age as David, Danny was one of the most convincing speakers David had ever known.

David had loved this man as a brother, now he just wanted to put a knife to Danny's throat and very slowly draw it across. They had studied together, roomed together, graduated together and worked together. They were inseparable until that dreadful event four years ago.

David sat for the rest of the morning wondering how he hadn't seen it coming. It seems so obvious now, but then he had trust. He trusted them all and that's why he didn't see the fuckers coming for him.

Licking his lips David realises he hasn't had a drink all morning, just coffee. He stands, and puts his coat on.

"Let's go get some lunch," he says to Shithead, and then he thinks "why take the creature?"

Anyone seeing him talking to his coat pocket will think he's crazy. Realising that most people expect the homeless to be a little crazy anyway, he picks up Shithead and puts it carefully in his inside coat pocket. The creature wriggles as it settles into the pocket.

"We need to beg some money for beer and food first."

He opens the front door which leads out to a small paved area at lower ground level. He is careful to jam the door shut without letting the latch catch since he has no key. He looks around sheepishly before climbing the stairs to street level.

David heads to his usual begging spot by Holborn Station. It was a good forty minutes walk at his shuffle, but he could beg en-route. In his usual spot his regulars would throw him ten or twenty pence sometimes even a fifty. It all added up and he always said "Thank you. You're a Godsend." On a good day he could make twenty pounds or more; on a bad day maybe two or three pounds.

Another bitterly cold day he was going to need a good day to get enough brew to see him through the night. He looks ahead at all the people scurrying about their day within close proximity to him yet deftly avoiding any kind of physical or eye contact with him. He was the same when he was one of them. The trick was to pick someone so preoccupied with their daily routine that they wouldn't notice his zombie like approach before being hit with a "fifty pence for a cup of tea please?" David looks ahead and sees a target. The man had just walked out of the revolving glass door of the office building holding a mobile phone. The man walks to the kerb looking at the phone intently as he waits for his car to pick him up. David goes into max shuffle trying to get to the man before his car arrives. As he approaches his mark he sees he is a young man in a very expensive looking grey coat. It's immaculate, probably new.

David reaches the still preoccupied mark and reaches out with his hand "Fifty pence for a cup of tea sir?" Startled, the young man turns quickly knowing what to expect.

"Don't touch me man! You're filthy," the young man is annoyed that he hadn't seen this tramp coming.

David had him. He doesn't like his lovely expensive clothing being touched. David reaches out again as if to stroke the man's arm. The man shifts away to his left reaching into his right outside coat pocket "Damn, no change. Just a note" he thinks to himself rummaging in the pocket.

"Look man, I've got no change; come back later."

"Got him" David thinks and wipes his running nose on the back of his hand then reaches out to the man again.

The man pulls the note out without even looking at it and throws it at David to repel the potential touch from the filthy vagrant. The note lands on the pavement and David moves like a ninja to retrieve it.

"Wow, a twenty" David pockets the note just as the man's car pulls up and he hurriedly gets in the back seat cursing the driver for being late. David can't believe his luck. The most he could have hoped for was a pound. He got a twenty note on his first mark.

"Well Shithead, we're going to drink well today" Shithead wriggles slightly in his coat pocket.

David heads to his usual mini-market where they do the six for £4 deal. Feeling elated he makes the fifteen minute walk in less than ten. He steps into the general store and is immediately greeted by a young Turkish man who shouts,

"Hope you got money man, no begging in here."

"I got money Saleem" David waves the twenty.

Saleem nods appreciatively. David heads to the beer fridge grabbing a basket on the way and slides open the fridge door. He picks up three four packs and heads to the checkout.

Saleem asks "Why you don't buy food and feed your body not rot your head and your liver?"

"I'm not here to buy advice Saleem just booze. How about I give you £6 for the twelve" David's feeling lucky.

"Yeah? And how about you explain that to my old man when he's kicking my arse" Saleem replies.

David chuckles and pockets his change. He is about to leave when he feels Shithead wriggling like crazy in his pocket. He grabs at the pocket.

"What the fuck you got in there man?" Saleem shouts "you know no animals allowed here."

David looks back at the checkout and suddenly feels the impulse to buy a lottery scratch card.

"How much for a scratch card?"

"These are two for two pounds one for one fifty. Now pay me pound and go," Saleem takes the money and gives David the tickets. David pockets the tickets and leaves the shop.

David is intrigued. He definitely felt as though he was compelled to buy the scratch cards. It was almost an uncontrollable desire, as if he had suddenly become addicted to the things. His stomach grumbles. He turns into an alley way and reaches into the bag for some refreshment. He cracks open a tin and drinks.

David heads back to his new flat to settle in for the rest of the day. At least he would be warmer than out in the open all day. He had enough tins and enough money for a McDonalds' meal. He picks up a quarter pounder with cheese meal, no drink, extra fries instead. David decides to wait till he gets back to the flat to eat the meal. He rushes to get to the flat before the meals gets cold wondering if Saleem had seen Shithead move under his coat, which must mean that it is real. Or maybe it was just the way he favoured that side of his coat pocket, which made it look as if he was hiding some kind of pet.

"Never mind, let's just get back and have some food" he speaks into his coat.

David arrives back at the flat and gives the front door a hefty shove to un-jam it. He shuts the door behind him and goes straight to the kitchen to check the electric meter; still eleven pounds and seventy five pence on it. No need to top it up yet. He goes into the bedroom and sits on the bed frame, reaches into his inside coat pocket and takes out a sleeping Shithead. He deposits Shithead on the pile of rags on the floor. Shithead stirs and opens its mouth licking its slitty lips. David pulls some fries out of the bag of food and feeds the fries to the eager Shithead. He feeds the creature till its mouth stops opening wanting for more. David then eats the burger and the remaining fries. With each bite of his food David thinks about his old friends. How could they? Why would they? Even if they had done what he suspects, what could he do? How can some broken down homeless alcoholic ever get close to these people who live in secure castles, to even have a conversation, let alone exact the type of revenge that he had started to imagine since last night's awakening? Burger and fries devoured, David washes it down with half a tin of brew and continues to ponder how he can get close to these people. In his condition he wouldn't get within fifty feet of any of them.

"How about we just jump one and hit em over the head and just keep bashing till they talk?" he asks Shithead.

The special brew kicking in nicely now. Shithead stirs. A sudden uneasy feeling comes over David. He feels an irresistible urge to reach into his coat pocket and take out the scratch cards. He feels for the tickets in his right external pocket and pulls them out. He then gets a ten pence coin out and looks at the first card. He looks at the card and starts to wonder which of the six squares he should start with. As he goes to scratch the top left square he suddenly knows that is the wrong square. He looks at the six options and knows exactly which three to pick. First, the top middle, he scratches away the grey covering and reveals a £ sign followed by 50,000. The amount registers, David continues to the square below the first. Another £50,000 revealed, next the square to the right of the second. He feels an odd sense of calm mingled with a suppressed sense of excitement. As he scratches at the third square his eyes widen as a £ followed by the number five appears then the rest. David stares at the card in disbelief.

He quietly whispers "Fifty thousand pounds," then louder "fifty thousand pounds!" He looks at the card again and again to make sure it's real. It's real alright. He quickly picks up the second card, but the same feeling which compelled him to buy and scratch off the first card holds him back. Instead he puts both cards back in his coat pocket. Four years ago this amount of money would have been a spit in the ocean, but now, but now this was life changing.

He looks down at Shithead "What the fuck are you? Is this real?" He scoops Shithead up and puts it in his pocket, grabs the bag of beer and heads for the front door. He leaves ensuring to jam the door shut just enough.

3 Blast from The Past

Three weeks after David's luck changed and fifty thousand pounds landed in his lap. He wakes up in a clean comfy bed. He reaches over to the pine bedside table and grabs a near empty bottle of Jack. He takes a big swig emptying the bottle.

"Three weeks ago I'd been reaching for a tin of beer in some alley somewhere" he thinks as he stares at the shoebox to the left of the bed.

Every morning he wakes up and looks at the box expecting it to be empty, not today.

"Big day today Shit; today we have some fun" David smiles and gets out of bed.

Same basement flat in Lexington Street, but now with some furniture and an equipped kitchen. Nothing fancy, just the basics so as not to attract any attention. Bed, small sofa, a little kitchen table and a chair. Functional small electric cooker with a washer dryer in the corner. The most important purchases were in a small cupboard in the bedroom. In the cupboard are the things that would allow him access to the people he wanted to see suffer. Expensive bespoke suit, shoes, shirts, ties and a five thousand pound Rolex. He'd spent over twenty thousand of the fifty so far. David showers, brushes his teeth and gets dressed.

One pm and Deepak Patel is behind his desk in his office situated above a ladies clothes shop on Duke Street in London's West End. He likes it here, easy access to shops and nightlife. Two things he considers essential in his life.

Deepak is a good looking man with the gift of coercion. He is aware of his looks and uses them to his advantage whenever he can. A very successful lobbyist, hired by large companies usually to influence Politicians and powerful Corporate Executives to find in favour of their interests. Danny recommended Deepak to David. He knew of a couple of companies that had used him with great success. David had Deepak checked out by Michael and Susan and he came up trumps.

Eight years success in his field, hated by some, respected by most including his competitors. Deepak's parents are typical in their expectations of their eldest son to forge a good career, get married and bear them grandchildren. The passing phase had been passing for the last twelve years. He however had no intention of marrying in the near or distant future and children will never be possible. At least not biologically.

A flat in the South Kensington area of London worth over two and a half million pounds, a car service on demand and the privacy to engage in his sexual activities without his parents or other family members displaying their disapproval. He knew at a very early age he was different. In the throes of puberty, instead of lusting after girls he found himself turned on by boys and men. He collected bodybuilding magazines to satisfy his desires to see the nude male form. He took up as many school sports which would allow him contact with other boys and satiate some of his desires. He had kept his affinity a secret from his younger brother and sister. At twenty five he plucked up the courage to come out to his family. They handled it in different ways. Some were appalled, some were sympathetic and others in denial. Deepak threw himself into his work; he liked the money and the freedom it bought him. He sees his family about once a month and this weekend is one of those feared visits.

Deepak looks at the clock on his desk. Lunch time, he gets up and grabs his coat from the stand and opens the door to his secretary's space.

"Popping to Gerard's Amy" he says to the young brunette as he rushes past her.

"OK Dee," Amy responds, continuing to stare at her monitor.

Deepak rushes down the stairs to the exit and opens the main door. He steps out and takes a deep breath. Ah, the smell of burnt hydrocarbons, the noise of the Capital and the sight of people in a rush to get somewhere. Gerard's is a men's clothes shop on New Bond Street and he sets off on foot to get there.

One hour later Deepak steps out of Gerard's with a bag in hand. As he steps out he walks into the path of a man. He is bumped off balanced; recovering he looks at the man, the man says

"Sorry," and he glimpses the man's face before the man turns to continue his journey. Deepak feels a bolt of dread shoot through him.

"Can't be" he mouths to himself, calming down.

Deepak looks at the stranger's back then shakes his head. He looks again. The stranger is gone.

"Naw, David was much fuller" he thinks as he walks back to the office.

Same day, a little later. Roger is outside a cafe near Bank Station. He is meeting with a Private Investigator who he hired to keep an eye on his wife Iris for the past month. The PI is Ian Draper, notorious for sniffing out cheating husbands and wives; his firm does brisk business out of suspicious spouses. At sixty four, Ian is a short chubby man with a full head of grey hair and slight stubble. Ian has done a lot of work for Roger and his colleagues in the past. He pulls a brown A4 envelope from his briefcase and hands them to Roger who looks at them with some degree of elation.

"She's just having tea with Linda and her husband" he states to Ian "I know she's clean. Nothing to worry about Roger, just trust the lady and enjoy your marriage." Roger hands back the photos to Ian.

"Thanks Ian" he pushes a white envelope over the table to Ian and gets up to leave. Just as he is standing up someone bumps him from behind.

"Sorry" the man says as he continues on. Roger gets a brief glimpse of the stranger's face and his heart sinks.

"David?" he asks looking at the stranger walking away.

He sets off in pursuit of the stranger, "Thanks!" Ian shouts as he pockets the envelope.

Roger barely hears Ian in his rush to catch up with the stranger.

"Hey, you in the black suit!" he shouts.

The stranger approaches Bank Underground Station and deftly takes the steps down. Roger's hefty frame and complete lack of fitness isn't helping him gain ground. He reaches the stairs and descends to the crowded ticket hall. He looks all around but there are so many men in black suits. He stands there for two minutes desperately looking for David yet hoping he was wrong.

Iris stands in front of the hotel room mirror looking at her shapely body. She had noticed a couple of grey hairs recently and this made her conscious of her age. At thirty four she was obsessed with staving off the aging process for as long as possible. Daily gym sessions and strictly controlled diet had kept her in fantastic shape. She looked more like a woman in her mid-twenties and she always enjoyed people complimenting her, especially men.

"You look amazing" the compliment comes from a voice behind her. She turns and looks at Danny who is lying naked in a tousled bed

"Better get dressed Danny, I'm expected back in the office by three" Iris says ignoring the compliment. She and Danny had been seeing each other for the last three years. With the amount of scrutiny Roger had her under they were only able to get together every two weeks for an hour or two. She was the best sex he'd ever had, insatiable, and dirty. She did things with her mouth that would make a man kill for. He was a better lover than Roger. Anyone was better than Roger. Roger had put on over four stones in the last three years. He was always hungry and food seems the only thing he is ever interested in. Iris liked sex, but preferred younger sturdier partners. Danny was just a release for her. He rarely got her to orgasm, but made up for that in the oral department.

Iris continues to dress in front of the mirror then pauses, "Do you ever wonder what happened to David?" she asks.

"No, he was no angel; he walked over more people than he ever helped. What we did was just business. I'm sure David saw it that way. I had him followed for a while after he walked out of the hearing. A homeless drunk was the last report. I imagine that status hasn't changed." Danny responds with an almost pre-rehearsed statement.

Danny Havers started out as a trainee stock broker straight out of University. A natural salesman he quickly rose up through the ranks and eventually after David had secured a controlling position with the Bank he asked him to join his merger team. Danny understood people. He could spot opportunities most would miss. Two years before the deed Danny started to plot. He saw the trust David had in his team and saw the greed in the team members including David. It was easy to manipulate everyone, play on their weaknesses and desires. The banking sector did one thing well. It created money hungry monsters that would do just about anything to keep the bonuses rolling in provided they could get away with it. Danny pulls back the sheet covering him and beckons to Iris,

"How about a quickie to keep the memory alive?"

"Just put your dick away and get dressed," Iris responds, hurrying to dress and make it back to the office before Roger. Iris finishes her makeup and grabs her hand bag.

"I'll email you about next week" she calls out as she exits the hotel room. She and Danny had created email accounts to allow them to communicate undiscovered using coded messages.

She takes the lift down to the lobby of the five star hotel in Kensington. Her car should be waiting. As usual she will get out three blocks before the office and walk the rest of the way. As she walks out of the hotel's revolving door she sees the car waiting. She gets in the back seat and tells the driver where to go. As the car pulls off she looks out of the left window and is startled by a smiling David standing on the pavement just looking at her. She shouts to the driver "Stop!" The driver brakes firmly ensuring the passenger is not thrown forward. Iris looks back at the spot she had seen David, but he's gone. Had she imagined it?

"Sorry, let's go" she tells the driver who looks a little puzzled.

Danny is checking out in the lobby. He finishes and heads to the revolving exit door. As he steps into the doorway he hears someone whisper "Hi Danny" behind him. He spins round just as the door encloses him.

He steps back and exclaims "Fuck me! David?"

Michael and Susan met while working for a large accountancy practice in York. They eventually set up their own company providing freelance services. David needed a small due diligence team which would report only to him so as to restrict any potential leaks. Michael and Susan fitted the bill. He hired them on a very favourable package.

Michael pushes back from his desk. It's 6pm and he has to leave early today. It's his mother's birthday and he has to get to the nursing home before visiting time finished. He picks up the small gift wrapped box and card from his desk and walks out of the office. Michael knocks on Susan's office door and opens it. He peeks in; Susan has her feet up on the desk reading a file as she always did.

"I'm off Sue" he says, wondering when she last tidied her desk.

"OK, wish Anne a happy one for me" she replies not even looking up.

Michael closes the door and heads to the lift. He gets in and presses the car park button. He loved being able to go straight down to the car park. So easy to just get in his car and drive the thirty minutes to the Sunset Care home in Wandsworth. There were still several cars parked, lots of people putting in the hours since the crunch. He reaches his car, a black Audi Q7. He gets in and drives off. Michael is a creature of habit. Same routine for every day of the week. He doesn't like change, which is all the more surprising that Danny was able to convince him to go against David. Today he would have worked till 7:30pm then visited one of his girlfriends. He allows himself a little smile thinking of his girlfriends.

Michael enjoyed the company of some of London's finest escorts. All he had to do was book his appointments online then just show up, pay his money and enjoy himself. The thought of all those beautiful women doing whatever he asked for in exchange for a bit of money without any of the emotional baggage that came with a relationship made him miss his usual visit, but it was his mother's birthday and dementia or not he was sure she would be looking forward to her present and card. Michael reaches the home and pulls into the car park. He enters the home and makes small talk with the nurse on reception then heads to his mother's room. When he gets to the room the door is open, which is standard practice. He enters and sees his mother sitting on her day chair.

"Happy Birthday mum" Michael puts on a cheery voice.

Anne looks up, "Ooh, another visitor, it must be my lucky day" she responds.

"You had another visitor?" Michael asks.

"Yes dear, he said he was your friend, even gave me a card" she points to the card on the dresser.

Michael walks over to the dresser and picks up the card.

It reads "Happy Birthday, Best Wishes David." Michael spins round and walks quickly to his mum

"Who gave this to you?" he asks.

"David dear; your friend David" Anne looks straight ahead. Michael knows better than to press further. He pulls out his phone and makes a call.

A busy side street in Soho. Its 7:15 pm and Susan approaches a well lit and colourful Chinese Restaurant. She opens the door to the Jade Garden Chinese restaurant.

"There my girl" a man's voice with a strong Chinese accent proudly proclaims. A smiling middle aged Chinese man approaches her and gives her a big hug, "you remember where the restaurant is at last" he continues to hug her.

"Dad, please. Where is mum?" Susan asks.

"At home, sulking. I said we can't go on holiday this year. Restaurant too busy, so she just walk off" he says rolling his eyes upwards.

"Dad, you both work hard all year, why don't you let Li run things for a week and take a break?" Susan asks feeling sorry for her long suffering mother.

"Cause it my business and I trust no one" he retorts, releasing his squeeze on Susan, "Now sit and have some dinner." Mr Chang gestures her to a table always reserved for family.

Susan Chang, the daughter of Chinese and Irish immigrants. This mix gave Susan very attractive facial features. Susan lacked any desire to be on trend in her sense of fashion. She had a scruffy appearance about her yet there was something there that couldn't quite be explained. With those exquisite dimples came a brilliant mind and an exceptional grasp of corporate accounts. As she sits she wonders where Danny might be tonight. She had suspected for some time now that he was playing around. She just hadn't taken the time to deal with it.

"Am I eating alone?" she looked at her father.

"No, no, just let me take this call first" she hadn't even noticed the phone ringing.

Susan goes back to thinking about Danny. He seemed so wonderful at first, and then over the past three years he had become progressively less attentive to her to the point where he barely notices her now. Danny used to be more careful about hiding his indiscretions, but lately he smelt of a particular perfume which Susan recognised. It was this that she wanted to discuss with Danny. Mr Chang returns mumbling something in Chinese.

"What's wrong dad?" she asks.

"Some comedian order a pile of food and there no one at the address where we deliver. When I find Mr Bloody Todd I give him black eye" Mr Chang vents.

Susan looks at her dad as he sits "Mr Todd?" she asks with an inquisitive look.

"Yeah Mr Bloody Todd" he responds, "Now let's eat." Susan's appetite rapidly fades.

The following morning after several concerned phone calls the night before, a meeting is arranged at Danny's office. They gather in the Investment Bank conference room discussing what they may or may not have seen the day before.

"It was him. That fucker's back. You said he was wallowing in some sewer, boozed up and broken" Roger looks directly at Danny.

Danny responds "You saw the video the PI took. He followed him for two years. All he ever did was beg, drink and sleep. He may have cleaned up and bought some second hand suit, but he's still a has been, piece of shit with no money and no way to touch us," remembering how close David had gotten to him. He could still feel David's breath on his neck. He felt a chill go through his body as he tries to reassure the others.

"Get your man back on the case. Let's find out where he is" Susan suggests.

"Hello, are we forgetting who we are talking about here. He is just letting us know he's back. We won't have to find him. He's coming to us. That disturbed fuck is handing out his business card" Deepak interjects.

Iris looks at Deepak "Don't be so fucking dramatic Deepak. He's just trying to scare us. He's got nothing on us, he's not the violent type plus his choice of weapon was always the pen, paper and litigation."

"He was in front of my mother for God's sake Iris. We don't know what state of mind he's in. I say we get the police involved" a worried Michael chirps up.

Danny shakes his head "The police? And say what? We briefly saw him, but can't be sure; he gave your mum a birthday card, on her birthday? Oh and the best one, Mr Todd ordered a prank home delivery. No fucking way, they will laugh at us. I think we go with getting the PI back on his trail, find him and confront him. Oh, this time we share the cost of the PI."

Roger usually has a constipated look on his face when he's about to say something stupid "Maybe we should talk to his wife. We still have tabs on her and if he has resurfaced, he's bound to get in touch with her."

Iris in a condescending tone "Sure he's going to try at making happy family again after what "He" she makes quote marks with her fingers "put them through. She's gonna welcome us and do her utmost to ensure we are safe too. No we just do the PI thing and wait to see what happens. In the meantime we keep vigilant and stay in contact with each other. He's probably sobered up and just wants to see what we are up to."

Deepak points out, "He was wearing a custom made suit. Not second hand and definitely not cheap, at least three grand. How the fuck can a down and out afford that?"

Danny gets up and starts to pace "I was sure that fucker would drink himself to death. Hell I even had someone ensuring he got enough from begging to keep the cheap booze flowing."

Susan looks up at Danny "You what? We bring him to his knees then you keep kicking?" a look of disgust crosses her face.

Danny raises his voice "Look, I made you all very rich and so far no one has complained. We all fucked David knowingly and eagerly. The only difference is that while you all walked away and just wanted to bury your heads in the piles of money I made you, I am the one who kept an eye on David to ensure he stayed fucking buried. It's been over four years now. Yes, I hoped he was dead; yes I facilitated his access to cheap booze, hell I hoped he would take to drugs." He pauses, looks at them and continues "Don't judge me when you're wearing a ten grand watch bought with money you'd never have had, but for me." Danny stares at them all with contempt and decides it's time to take charge "We all go about our business as usual. If he surfaces again, then try to get a photo and let the rest know immediately. If possible try to find out what he wants. I'll instruct the PI. We have a merger to put to bed, now everyone fuck off out and do your jobs" Danny opens the door beckoning them out.

Same day 3:30 pm. David sits in a mini-cab on a quiet side street in Clapham watching a house about one hundred meters away. His eyes tear up as he sees a woman pull up in front the house in an old blue Volvo. The woman gets a carrier bag out of the rear passenger seat and goes to the front door of the house. He wants to get out of the car and rush over to her, but he knows better. Their last exchange of words was about his greed and the culture of greed that he had helped to cultivate which led to the sorry state that they were in. He knew the culture created by the banking environment had led to his downfall and she was pulled down with him. She had warned him time and time again, but he was blinded by his desire to 'acquire' as she put it. A tear rolls down his cheek. He wipes it away and says to the driver "Let's go."

Mary King, she took back her maiden name before the ink on the Decree Absolute was even dry. She worked part time in a small solicitor's office as a legal secretary and had spent the past three years creating a new life for her and her sons. The house in Hampstead was gone and now she was living in a rented accommodation with a little help from the Council. It wasn't a dream life, but it was peaceful and honest. Every now and then she would think about David and wonder what he was doing.

Thoughts of David generally made her angry and resentful. Mary entered the house and says to herself "Better get dinner ready before they get home."

4 Superbia

Deepak opens the door to his Kensington two bedroom apartment. His home epitomises good taste. He had spent a lot of time and money to create a modern look where he could entertain friends. His mobile rings. He checks to see who is calling. It's his mother.

"Hi Mum, everything OK?" he steadies himself for what's to come.

"We could be dead and you wouldn't even know" his mum starts.

Deepak rolls his eyes upward "Here we go" he thinks to himself, always ten minutes of whinging before she can get to the real reason for the call.

He wasn't in the mood today for a lecture on family and responsibilities.

"Mum, please, I've had a really bad day and just want to relax now. Is there something wrong?" Deepak asks sternly.

Sensing the seriousness in his voice his mum gets to the point "We are entertaining Mr and Mrs Amin tomorrow. Their daughter is a lovely girl and she is coming too. We thought you might like to come over and spend some time getting to know her."

Here we go, always trying to get him married,

"Mum, what part of I'm gay don't you understand? I don't think Mr and Mrs Amin's daughter will be the magical cure you are both hoping for. I won't be coming. I'm sorry to disappoint you" Deepak hopes this will stop her, but she continues.

"Dee you are a successful young man, but one day you will wake up and regret not starting a family. Now, you are still my son and I expect you to put up with us for just one night. I will see you tomorrow night." With that she puts the phone down.

Deepak takes a shower and dresses for a well needed night out. Feeling in a somewhat dark mood he goes for all black. Well mostly black. Black suit, grey shirt, no tie and black shoes. He glances at his watch, 8pm; the arrangement for the evening was to meet up with three friends for dinner then on to a wine bar for drinks. He grabs his keys, wallet and phone leaves.

David stands huddled in a recessed doorway where he has a good view of Deepak as he leaves the apartment building. Deepak gets into a waiting car. David is dressed in his street clothes with his face covered by a scarf. As Deepak's cab pulls off he steps out and approaches the apartment building. He says something to the doorman and the doorman lets him in.

Deepak arrives at Lumins, a Pan Asian restaurant popular with the rich and famous and wannabe rich and famous.

The head waiter greets him "Dee, good to see you again. Your friends are here."

The waiter leads him to his usual table.

"Thanks Kim" Deepak pats him on the shoulder and turns his attention to the three people sitting at the table.

"Deb, James, Will" he greets.

"You three look a bit sheepish, been talking about me again?" Dee asks.

Deb is a short brunette with shoulder length hair. She is wearing a white open necked blouse tucked into a knee length blue skirt. James is tall and skinny. Always dressed in a suit jacket with mismatched trousers, he is aware of his slender frame. The stubble is a deliberate attempt to man up. Will is one of Deepak's oldest friends and the only one at the table who knew of Deepak's sexuality from a very early age. Will is much like Deepak, good looking and sharply dressed.

"What's the plan tonight?" Dee asks already knowing the answer.

Will replies "Usual, eat, drink and get laid."

"I have an early start tomorrow, can't be up too late" Dee says.

Deb looks at Dee "You mean Politicians to bribe and all that?"

"No one likes a cynical bitch Deb" the defence comes from James.

"We create symbiotic relationships which are beneficial to the general public and commerce" Dee slips into work mode.

Will jumps in "Ease up on the speeches Dee; we are here to have some fun, now who's for some hard stuff?" They all laugh and settle down for a good evening out.

8am the next morning. Dee slowly opens his eyes. His head really hurting, his vision is blurry and his tongue is dry as hell.

"What the fuck happened?" he thinks, desperate to remember why his head is hurting so bad. He'd been drunk many times before but this was a different kind of hangover. The room is dark, but he knows it's his flat. He quickly turns to look at the bedside clock. 8:01am, he should have been at the Houses of Parliament at 7:30. He tries to sit up, but it's like trying to move in a bowl of thick porridge.

"Hello Dee" a familiar voice from across the room.

Dee peers into the darkness, a lamp is switched on and Dee comes out of the haze instantly. "David? What the fuck you doing here?"

David is sat in a cosy chair. He just stares at Dee not speaking. Dee desperately tries to get up, but his body feels paralysed.

"What have you done to me?" he asks, the panic in him growing by the second.

David doesn't answer. He sits there savouring every moment. The look of panic on Dee's face as he wrestles to overcome the feeling of paralysis.

Dee pleads "David please, I can give you money, just give me a chance please."

David stands up and walks towards the bed slowly, watching Deepak intently "How much money do you think it will take to make up for what my friends did to me? How much do you reckon Dee?" David's voice is cold, devoid of emotion.

Dee is scared "P...Please David, I... I can't move." Deepak stutters "I've got over 15 mill in cash and another 2 in stocks. You can have it all just please don't do anything to me."

"What do you think I'm going to do to you Dee?" David still watching him with a dispassionate stare.

"Look, my laptop is on the desk, I can arrange a transfer now" Deepak tries to calm down and rely on what he does best. Talk people round to his way of thinking.

"Ok Dee, let's say I accept your offer, what happens when I leave this flat? You call the police, I get arrested and the money is returned to you."

"No I promise, I won't say a thing. You can trust me." Deepak uses his most sincere voice.

"Like I trusted you when you and my other friends pulled my trousers down and fucked me silly" David lets out a wry laugh. He walks back to the chair and sits "You've got a great place here, must be worth well over 2 million. Great place, expensive clothes, you really take a lot of pride in yourself and surroundings Dee. You always have. Maybe that's why you fucked me. You had to feed your pride with more things" David spits the words out, anger now evident in his voice.

Dee starts to defend his actions "It wasn't like that."

David shouts "It was just like that!" he takes a deep breath and calms down. He wants to be in control so he can enjoy what's to come. He gets up and approaches Deepak. David walks up to the bed and leans in to be face to face with Deepak. He sits on the bed.

David calmly "You all knew what you were doing. What it would do to me, my family, my career, but none of you gave a shit. The millions that you all made was the only thing you cared about," he strokes Dees face with his right index finger, "now I'm going to show you there is more to life than just money. There is life itself. I had the takeover of Genova Technology sewn up. We needed those votes to get the go ahead for the purchase of the licences for the for the new generation wireless chip. The defence contracts were in place. Everything was in place and agreed. The vote was a foregone conclusion; somehow you got enough MPs to change their minds and vote against it. Tell me Dee what did you offer them to get them to change? Money, shares, what?"

Deepak tries to raise his arm to grab David. His arm rises slowly and fumbles at David's shirt collar. His mind racing to find a solution. Despite David's calm voice Deepak sees the madness in his eyes. This is not the man he knew before. David gets off the bed and walks back to the chair. He sits.

"Money" Dee whispers.

"How much?"

Deepak takes a breath "Two hundred thousand each."

David shakes his head and lets out a heavy sigh "I know what you're thinking. Your office will be wondering where you are. The neighbours will hear the shouting. Thing is, you called your secretary last night and left a message to cancel your 7:30 and you'd be taking the day off. As for the neighbours, they're like you, out early back late. We should be finished by then" David watches Dee for a reaction.

"Finished what?" Deepak asks not really wanting to hear the answer.

David looks at Dee and tilts his head slightly to the right "Well, it's always hard when you lose a loved one. Some people handle it well some don't. You look like the "don't" type."

"What the fuck are you talking about, I've lost no one" Dee replies.

"Really, what about poor Simon?" David waits for the question

"Simon? Who the fuck is Simon?" Dee can't see where this is going.

"Simon is your boyfriend and he died last night" David lifts his left arm and points to the floor on the other side of the bed. Dee uses all his strength to lean over to where David is pointing. As he flops to the other side of the bed he begins to convulse. The shock is almost beyond what he can bear. There, beside the bed, is the body of a young man. Pale and grey. A needle hanging out of his arm and most definitely fucking dead. His eyes wide open just staring upward. Dried foam around his mouth and completely naked. Dee is crazy with fear now. He wants to vomit, but can't. He starts to tremble with fear and shock. David killed this man. Now he is going to kill him.

"You picked up Simon last night in a pub in Kennington. You two had a very vigorous evening from what I saw. It must have been hard keeping your secret from all your family in the early days. If only they knew how much you fuck around what do you think they would say?" David's voice becomes more taunting.

"You, fuck... you... f..." Dee is on the verge of a fit.

David jumps up moves swiftly to the bed, grabs Deepak and sits him up in the bed.

"Can't have you choking on your tongue or whatever that is coming out of your mouth is now after all the effort I've gone to" David sits back down. Deepak's face sinks, he can't even think of what to say. His first dead body. My God he's next.

Dee looks up slowly "Please you can have it all just let me live, please?" Dee is drooling now and tears are streaming down his face. His body shakes with fear. His mind reels with thoughts of what he can say or do to put a stop to this madness unfolding in his own bedroom.

David is in full flow. He thought it would feel good, but this was so much better than he ever expected. He feels in complete control, in this place he is God. He remembers a time when he felt this way before. He had missed it. He looks at Dee's pathetic face. The smarm and bravado completely exorcised from his persona. David is ready to deliver the next blow.

"As I was saying, what would your family think of you, the jewel in the crown, if they knew the life of promiscuity and debauchery that you live? Well, being the kind of guy that I am and knowing how much you and Simon meant to each other I thought I should introduce Simon to them since you are so shy in coming forward." David looks at Dee to make sure he is still conscious. Deepak's eyes are glassy, the shock of what is happening has sent him into a place he has never been before; a place where he has absolutely no control and no hope of ever getting even the slightest drop on a man intent on killing him. David could probably stop here and leave Dee a veg for the remainder of his life. David reaches over to the bedside table and picks up a glass of water. He gives Dee a sip. Dee comes to a little more.

"That's better; you need to be awake for the next bit." David walks over to a table near the cosy chair with the laptop. He picks up the laptop and goes back to the bed. He sits beside

Dee and pushes the power button on the laptop. It's an instant on machine.

David stares at the screen "Your problem is you never had the balls to tell your family once and for all that you had zero intentions of satisfying their expectations of you. Now see that camera on the desk?" Deepak looks up, definitely recovering now. "Well let's say you and Simon did your own "Balls and Wood" movie last night, and lucky for you I was the Director and Cameraman" David clicks on the Media player. Dee's eyes widen and he starts to breathe rapidly again.

"What have you done! What the fuck have you done!?" Dee is now wide awake watching himself sucking Simon's dick. Close up.

"There plenty more" David says "You fucking him, him fucking you, cum everywhere, in your mouth, ass, everywhere Dee, regular cumfest."

Deepak is crying hard now "Please David, don't do this it will destroy my family" Deepak splutters as he breathes rapidly trying to move his arms to brush the laptop off the bed.

"Did you know you can upload a video file to a website like the one I started last week in your name; I called it Ilovedicknotpussy.co.uk. Great name ha? Surprisingly the only video on there is this one. Anyway, now that you are a movie star, I thought we should share your talents with all your family. Then I thought why stop there? Let's send a link to everyone in your contacts."

David looks at Dee's face. The man is sobbing, tears rolling down, snot running, convulsions the lot, "Stay with me Dee, I want you to push the button to send the email with the link to the site. I've got it ready."

David holds Dee's left hand and pulls it towards the laptop. He holds his index finger and steers it towards the touch screen.

Dee struggles to pull away, but he has no strength. "Come on Dee, just a few seconds now and you are famous!" Dee's finger touches the screen the email is sent. He shakes his head. Please let this be some bad nightmare, maybe he'll wake up any second now in his room alone and safe.

"Now, just three things more to sort out and I can leave. First I have to thank you for the transfer you did last night." David pauses for the response.

"What transfer?" Dee looks puzzled.

"The one we did before you and Simon turned porn stars. The fifteen mill" David smiles as he watches the remaining blood drain out of Dee's face.

All this time he had the money. Dee knows now he will die this morning. David has already killed the man on the floor what's to stop him taking another life

"Are you going to kill me?" Dee asks.

"No not me. You are. You see, Simon was an old friend of mine from the streets. His big problem was heroin. He'd fuck and suck anyone for the money to buy it. That's probably how he became HIV positive. After last night I'm pretty sure you have joined the club Dee." Dee expels a long breath and closes his eyes. Yesterday his life was on track. A track of his making.

David keeps talking "I've bought you a new accessory for your punching bag hook in the guest room. You'll see it, in a little while." David's excitement mounts.

Dee's phone starts to ring, David picks it up. "Hey, it's your mum; guess she's seen the vid" David chuckles. He puts the phone down and continues to let Dee in on his plan. The phone continues to ring and flash.

"In about five minutes you will be able to walk again. You will stand up and go to the spare room. In there is a noose attached to the punching bag hook. You are going to stand on the stool below the hook, put your head through the noose and kick the stool away" David stops and waits for Dee to stop sobbing.

Dee's phone rings again, it's his brother.

"Popular boy today Dee" David taunts "it's a shame about Simon, but he is in a better place now. Don't think he would have survived much longer the way he was shooting up. At least I gave him a hotel room and a good last few days."

"You won't get away with this. The others will call the police the minute they find out. They know you're back" Dee's hopes are gone.

He doesn't know why, but he wants to go into the room. He starts to feel his arms and legs again, but instead of attacking David he just wants to do what David says. The time ticks by and Deepak starts to feel more of his legs and arms. He swings his legs slowly off the bed avoiding Simon's body. He pushes hard upwards with his legs and stands. No matter how much he tries not to obey David he cannot resist and continues to head towards the bedroom door. David follows him, saying nothing, savouring every moment. Deepak exits the bedroom and slowly walks to the guest room. He tries hard to stop moving, to throw himself to the floor to move his arms, but nothing; Just the slow relentless march to his beautifully decorated guest room. Deepak reaches the spare room. The door is open. He enters and sees David's handy work. He's crying hard. David enters the room and stands in the doorway watching. Dee approaches the stool. He gets up on it and turns to face David. Still crying he puts his head into the noose. He looks at David hoping for some kind of reprieve. None, David's face is lit with excitement. Dee kicks the stool away to the rear. There is a harrumph sound as the rope kicks in. Dee's body flays around violently. His face goes purple, his tongue swells and protrudes from his open mouth. Piss runs down his naked leg. His body loses control completely and shit runs to the floor. The trashing stops. Slight convulsions then fewer and fewer till Deepak's body hangs lifeless. David smiles, turns and walks away.

Back at Lexington Street David opens the shoebox

"One less" he says looking at the creature. He peers a little closer. Only two fingers on Shithead's right arm now.

5 Gula

Eight thirty am Roger is at his office desk. His mobile phone rings. It's Susan. A very hyper Susan speaks "Roger, my god have you seen the video?"

"What video" Roger asks.

"The one Dee sent to just about the entire planet. Dee did a home sex video and put it on the net. Check your email" Susan's voice gets higher.

"Hang on" Roger grabs his PC mouse. He opens the email from Dee and clicks on the link. "Holy shit! What the fuck is this idiot thinking? This will destroy him. Have you called him?"

"Tried a few times, no answer. He called in sick at his office too. Maybe he was pissed or on drugs" Susan postulates.

Roger thinks then tells Susan "I'll go to his apartment. See if he's there."

"Ok call when you get there" Susan hangs up.

Roger gets up and rushes out of his office. He calls Dee's office number on his mobile while fussing to get his overcoat on.

"Hi Amy, what's going on with Dee?"

A distraught Amy responds "I don't know, but after seeing this I'm guessing we are out of business. I don't know what got into Dee, but it's going to ruin us Roger. What am I going to do?"

"I'm heading over to his flat, where does he keep the spare key Amy?"

"It's with the concierge. The password is 'silk'."

Roger ends the call and waddles as quickly as he can to the waiting taxi outside his office building. He gets into a black cab and tells the driver the address. The taxi sets off. Roger looks out the cab window. Shop windows decked out for the Christmas shopping season. They say people can go a little loopy this time of year, but Dee. Not Dee. He was always too disassociated to care about anything but himself.

The taxi arrives at Dee's apartment. Roger gets the key from the Concierge and takes the lift up to Deepak's floor. He gets out and approaches Deepak's apartment. He rings the door bell. No response. He presses the button again and shouts "Dee, it's Roger, open up. Dee." No response. Roger uses the key and opens the door "Wow, that's funky" the stink hits him hard. He reaches for the light switch. The lights come on along the hallway; he looks up the hallway. There is light on in one of the bedrooms. The door is open and some kind of shadow is formed on the floor. The shadow is moving slightly to one side then the other. Roger approaches "Dee, that you? Stop fucking about. Dee?" No answer. Roger reaches the doorway. The smell is stronger now. He turns into the room entrance

"Holy shit!" Roger is repelled.

Half an hour later Dee's apartment is filled with police, and people in white overalls and masks. Roger is sitting in Dee's living room. Shaken and still incredulous, Roger is being interviewed by a policewoman.

"The body in the bedroom, from the note left on the laptop it looks like that was Mr Patel's boyfriend. Looks like he overdosed and your friend took his own life in his grief," the policewoman tries to explain to Roger. Roger looks at the policewoman. She is in plain clothes, wearing a ladies suit and trousers. She has a stern no nonsense look about her. She is about thirty five, but could be mistaken for forty two.

Roger "No, if you knew Dee, you'd know how improbable that theory sounds."

"Mr Caldwell, there are no signs of foul play and the amount of drugs lying around the bedroom would indicate that Mr Patel and his friend were pretty high when all this happened. We are still trying to ID the other body. There's nothing in here to tell who he was. There will be an autopsy and forensics are still at work, but unless you know otherwise, I strongly suspect this will be classed as a suicide and or drug overdose."

The policewoman touches Roger's hand "Do you want me to arrange a taxi for you?" Roger ignores the question.

"What about his parents? Have they been told?" Roger asks.

"Yes, they are on their way now. I think its better you go home and if we need to speak with you again we will call," the Policewoman suggests.

Roger has other plans. He needs to get the others together and figure out if David was involved. Roger takes the lift and gets out into the Foyer. He sees an old Indian couple coming towards him. The woman is inconsolable; the man has his arm around her. Dee's parents. Roger realises he's never met them before. That's how secretive Dee was about his private life. Maybe the body by the bed was his boyfriend. Roger walks past the grieving couple and out to the pavement. He hails a black cab and sets off to the office.

Another hastily arranged meeting in the conference room of the Investment Bank; only five people this time are sat at the table.

Danny is quite agitated "Look this is just a coincidence. Dee had a very private life. We don't know what he got up to at nights. He lurked in many dark places to get information and leverage on others."

A still shaken Roger asks Danny "Did you speak with Draper? Is he looking?"

Danny looks at Roger "Yes I spoke to him, but he can't start till tomorrow."

Michael speaks up "What do we do now? If David is having some kind of breakdown coupled with murderous intent then we're all in danger" the room falls silent.

Susan "Either we all go to the police and explain that it might be David who is responsible, or wait to see if anything else happens. Personally, I can't imagine David being involved in something like this. I think Danny is right. It is a coincidence."

Roger shakes his head "So we just do nothing and wait to see if he strikes again. Great plan; In that case I have a 4 o'clock contract review meeting I need to get to. Can I suggest that we stay in touch every two hours for the remainder of this day?"

"Sounds good" agrees Michael.

They all get up and leave with the exception of Danny. Danny gets up and walks to the conference room window "Where are you David?"

Roger arrives at Luigi's Italian restaurant in Shoreditch. He enters and is greeted by the Headwaiter

"Good afternoon Mr Caldwell, your usual table?"

Roger "Yes please Andrew."

Andrew leads Roger to a table against the far left wall. Nice and secluded for private conversations. He sits and orders a Whiskey and Soda. Before the drink can arrive the two men he is meeting approach the table led by Andrew.

"Griff, Jason" Roger stands up and shakes hands with the men.

The men are very similar looking. Middle aged, suited and grey hair. Jason is wearing spectacles. Griff is a short thin man and Jason about a foot taller and a little fuller build.

"Drink gents?" Roger asks.

Jason orders for both men "Please, I'll have a Jack and coke large and Griff will have a pint of lager. Now what's good in here?"

Roger responds "The steaks are the best. Especially the fillet"

Jason is convinced "Ok we'll have two of those medium rare with fries and salad. Better get a nice bottle of the red stuff"

"Easy to see who's in charge between these two" Roger thinks to himself. Roger orders the same meal. The waiter departs with the order and Roger gets his meeting folder out. The men engage in discussion, order a couple more drinks and are happy when the food arrives.

Roger closes his folder "I will make the agreed changes and bike the final draft to you tomorrow for approval."

Jason smiles "Great, now let's eat."

The men set about their late lunch or early dinner making small talk. Usual stuff, family, holidays, work. Roger starts to feel a little warm. He sips at the wine and glances across at Jason's plate. Out of nowhere comes the thought "His fries look crispier than mine" Roger shakes his head slightly, discarding the thought. He glances at Jason's plate again all the while maintaining chit chat. Roger wants to try one of Jason's fries. His left hand, armed with a fork, starts to tremble slightly. Roger has an irresistible desire for some of the lovely golden, crispy fries on Jason's plate. "Why are his fries so much crispier looking than mine?" he thinks to himself. Suddenly Roger reaches out to Jason's plate and stabs a few fries with his fork, pops them in his mouth and eats. They are as crispy and tasty as he imagined. Roger thinks "Did I really just do that?"

Jason is surprised. He looks at Roger "Hey, no problem plenty to go round." Roger is starting to sweat slightly. That thin sheen of sweat that appears on your face and forehead when you feel flushed and flustered.

Roger apologises "I'm so sorry Jason, I don't know why I did that" but before he can conclude his apology his hand shoots out and does it again.

Jason "Roger just because your firm is paying for this doesn't mean you have to eat it all"

Roger wants to get up. The feeling is getting worse. As he munches on the second lot of fries, he looks at Griff's plate "Why is his steak so much juicier and tender looking than mine?"

Roger thinks to himself "No, please no!"

Then it happens, Roger just helps himself to a thick slice of steak and washes it down with Griff's wine. Both men are incredulous.

Jason now pissed off, pushes his chair back and stands up

"If this is how you treat your clients, you can go to hell. I'll find someone else. No wonder you're so fucking fat."

Both men collect their coats and leave. Roger is still sat at the table eating. He continues to eat till all three meals are finished. Roger sits staring at the empty plates. What just happened? How could he lose control like that? Stuffed and bloated he decides to go home.

Andrew is concerned "Is everything OK Mr Caldwell?"

Roger mumbles "Yeah fine" takes his coat and leaves.

At 6:00 pm Roger arrives at his four bedroom detached house in Hampstead Heath not far from where David used to live. He and Iris bought it when they married with the intention of starting a family, but forging a career was first priority for them both and as time slipped by the conversation became non-existent. It was a new build with all the mod cons a successful professional couple could want. Large well decorated rooms.

Highly specified kitchen and bathrooms, and a very high price to accompany it all. Roger's stomach is hurting a little from his late lunch, yet out of instinct and habit he goes to the kitchen, opens the fridge and looks for something sweet to eat.

"What the hell is wrong with me?" he asks himself quickly closing the fridge door. He wants to walk away from the kitchen, but can't. He opens the door again. He glimpsed a slice of chocolate cake and just wants a taste. He needs to taste this cake. Roger takes the cake out and sits at the kitchen table and eats the slice of cake. Very full, now he needs a nap.

Roger awakes from a drowsy sleep. He is still sitting at the kitchen table face down on it. As he becomes aware of where he is, he hears a familiar voice at the other end of the table.

"Hello Roger."

The voice sinks in and his stomach suddenly gripes. Instant recall of what happened to Dee flashes through his mind. It's David. He peers through blurry eyes straining to focus on the figure at the other end of the table. It's David for sure. He's just sitting there looking quite different from before they fucked him. A bit older, thinner and somewhat sallow.

Roger tries to compose his thoughts. Just because David is here in his kitchen sat opposite him as he awakes doesn't mean he is here to do him harm. Roger needs to delude himself if he is to maintain the control needed to gain control of the situation. He's sure that he can reason with him; offer him something that Dee hadn't thought of.

"David, let's talk about this. I know what we did was wrong, but a lot of money came out of it. I can give you half of what I made" Roger's mind kicks in.

"A very tempting offer, but I have a partner who is less interested in money and more in retribution" David says peering at Roger wondering when he will notice the contents of the kitchen table.

Roger is sure he can make David see the benefit of profit over whatever else he has in mind for him

"Then let me meet with your partner, we can all discuss how to come to a compromise that ends well for all."

The kitchen table is six feet by four feet. David gestures with his head to the table then looks up and says "I know you are usually quite peckish so I brought you a little snack." Roger takes in the contents of the table. It's laden with a variety of junk food. Two large deep pan pizzas, four quarter pounders with cheese, a fourteen piece KFC bucket, fish and chips, apple pie and two extra large dirty kebabs. "Looks good huh?" David asks with a little smile.

Roger feels slightly sick "I'm really not hungry. Had a lot to eat earlier. I can move two million to you today, more later. Let's just discuss this please?"

David stands and walks round the table approaching Roger. He sits on a chair to the left of Roger. He leans towards Roger and quietly says "I don't know Roger. I put my trust in you and the others and you used that trust against me. I never even thought about looking over the merger contract, because I had a crack team which included one of the City's finest Corporate Lawyers to ensure that this campaign went as smoothly as the countless others before. You drew up a second set of contracts didn't you?"

"Please David, give me a chance to make this good" Roger pleads. David moves slightly closer to Roger and whispers "How much do you trust the others? How much do you trust Danny or your wife?" Roger looks into David's eyes. He sees the menace in them. He realises now that there is no negotiating his way out of this. David continues "I know you suspect Iris is fucking around, I know you had that ex-cop follow her, taking pictures. None of which have proven her guilt. A bit odd don't you think? A woman like her with needs that you can't even begin to satisfy must be fucking around. Well I thought I'd help you out with this. I had a little chat with Ian earlier. Turns out he's quite the pal with Danny."

David gets up quickly and almost skips over to a kitchen work surface to pick up some overturned A4 size photographs. He sits at the table again and places the photos in front of Roger with a look of excitement on his face. Roger looks at the first photo. He looks away, tears welling up. The photo shows Iris being fucked doggy style by Danny on some hotel room bed.

"Looks like Ian took photos, but bullshit you on Danny's say so. Looks like Ian kept the real stuff in case he needed some leverage over Danny. Can't trust anyone these days, can you?" David says closely observing the mental anguish he is inflicting on Roger. He proceeds to show the other photos to Roger. One by one he flips them. David smiles "Here is a good one, notice how she is able to swallow his entire penis. Man that girl is good" he flips to the next "This is one of my favourites. See how comfortable she is on top. Can she do that on you and still reach your dick?" Roger looks away "Look at the pictures Roger!" David's voice is stern and commanding.

Crushed, Roger looks at the pictures weeping "You bastard David" he sobs.

David looks at the pictures "Do you think this is my doing? Not me Roger. It's not my dick in your wife's mouth in this picture. It's not me slipping away from the office every other week to fuck Danny. You disgusting parasites are now feeding on each other." David pauses and leans back in his chair. He wants to savour every moment of Roger's misery. With a slight smile he says "Don't worry. I have something special planned for

Iris." Roger doesn't react to this. David continues "Now this tragic disclosure must make you want to comfort eat. How about a nice slice of pizza?"

Roger, still weeping "I'm not hungry."

"Eat!" David commands.

Roger is unable to resist the urge to pick up a slice of pizza. He reaches out, picks up a thick cheese laden slice and takes a bite. Then another, and another. He finishes the slice. His stomach is achingly full.

"Keep eating!" David's voice rings in his ears again.

"I can't, I'm full, ate too much earlier" Roger says trying to breathe. He is so full the pressure from his enlarged gut is pushing upwards on his lungs.

"Eat you gluttonous fat pig" David orders.

Roger picks up another slice starts eating. With each bite he feels his stomach expand. His hands keep pushing the thick slab of cold solidified slab of cheesy bread into his mouth and his mouth keeps chewing. He cannot stop eating. He feels much like someone drowning only instead of water he is drowning in food. He finishes all the pizza and turns his attention to the burgers. Roger's stomach is on the verge of bursting. As he struggles to breathe he takes only small sharp breaths as he crams more food into his mouth. Bite after bite he continues. Getting fuller and fuller expecting his gut to explode any moment. His engorged stomach desperately trying to accommodate the onslaught of food. He wants to be sick, he wants to vomit but the reflex doesn't kick in. He just keeps picking up food and shoving it into his mouth. David just watches wondering if his stomach will burst soon, fascinated by the capacity of the man. Roger has finished two thirds of the food.

"Stop!" David orders "I've got a very special dish for you. Have you ever heard the expression 'Don't bite the hand that feeds you?"

Roger gasps as his hands stop pushing a piece of apple pie into his already stuffed mouth. He spits the contents of his mouth out.

David leans forward and slowly repeats his question "Have you heard the expression "Don't bite the hand that feeds you?"

Roger still struggling to breathe answers "Yes, yes."

David continues "Good. I made you a very rich man, but that wasn't enough, you had to rob me. Not let's examine that phrase a further. You bit my hand now it's your turn to see what it feels like." David leans in closer to Roger. Instantly Roger thinks David is going to bite him. He tries to move back, but can't. There is no space on the chair for him to move back. Then David says "I want you to eat your left hand Roger."

Roger desperate for air splutters "No, please no, you can have it all, all the money, please David"

"Eat your left hand" David repeats in a slow calm voice.

Powerless to resist, Roger looks at his left hand. He fights against the desire to move his hand to his face, but to can't. Nose running and crying hard now, he puts his thumb in his mouth. He bites down slowly. Excruciating pain shoots through his thumb, but he doesn't stop. He bites through the skin then the flesh to the bone. The pain is unbearable. He crunches down hard on the bone cracking it and teeth in the process. He rips loose the thumb from his hand with his teeth and continues to chew at the thumb trying to reduce it so he can swallow. David watches closely, enjoying the pain and humiliation he is inflicting on this man who he so hated. Roger manages to break down some of the thumb and tries to swallow. Sharp bits of bone hack at his throat as he swallows, cutting and ripping as it tries to go down. Roger's mouth is awash with blood, his hand bleeding profusely. He raises his hand to his mouth and goes for the index finger. David watches as this man who he once called a friend, who came to his house for dinner parties, who he allowed to play with his kids, the same man who he now takes sadistic pleasure watching, suffer in this way. As a bleeding, crying Roger finishes the appendage David stops him.

"No, you must be full by now. I bet you must be just about bursting right now. Imagine releasing all that pressure on your stomach. Is that what you want?" David asks. Roger is a complete mess, unable to answer and afraid of what could possibly come next. The pain in his hand, throat, mouth and stomach now so bad that death would be a good option.

David continues "Under the napkin to your right is a very sharp knife. Now wouldn't it feel nice to slip that knife into your belly and pull it across till your guts fall out? That will make you feel better."

Roger raises the napkin and sees one of his treasured expensive super sharp Santoku kitchen knives. He remembers the Teleshopping advert which convinced him that he needed a set of indestructible super sharp kitchen fucking knives. He pops open the buttons on his shirt easily with his still intact right hand. He pulls the shirt open, picks up the knife and positions it to the left of his belly.

David whispers "Look at me."

Roger knows it's over now. His cheating wife will come home and find him like this. He pushes the knife into his belly and slowly draws it across. He gets midway and there is a gushing sound as his stomach sac forces its way out followed by intestines. They land on his lap. He looks down and sees his guts gush from the slit onto his lap then slide and slip tothe kitchen floor. He's still alive as his right hand continues on its merciless journey across his belly as his eyes shut and his body goes limp. David smiles as he stands and walks to Roger's study.

David returns home. He goes into the bedroom and pulls a shoebox out from under the bed. He looks at Shithead. Only one finger on the right arm now.

6 Ira

Ian Draper rings the doorbell of Mary King's house. He had managed to conclude his other business and thought he may as well get an early start on locating David. The curtain in the bay window to the right of the door moves slightly. Ian rings the bell again. A voice comes through the closed door.

"Who is it?" asks a wary Mary.

"My name is Ian Draper, I'm a Private Investigator, I'd like to talk to you about David Todd" Ian replies.

"I don't want to talk about David Todd. I closed that chapter in my life and do not want to reopen it" Mary's voice is very calm. She opens the door.

Mary looks at Ian; he's holding some sort of ID showing his PI licence.

"That means nothing to me" she looks him in the eye.

Ian "Have you seen David lately?"

Mary "No, now go away, my kids are upstairs getting ready for school. I don't want them hearing that name."

Ian "There have been some strange things happening to some of your ex-husband's old work colleagues. I wondered if David has tried to make contact with you. Perhaps you know where he stays?"

Mary "Listen Mr Draper, I don't give a fuck where or what he is doing. I don't give a fuck about his old so called buddies and frankly I don't take kindly to you turning up on my doorstep asking questions. So please take this the right way and fuck off" she slams the door shut.

Ian turns and walks back to his car.

Michael Howard is a devoted son who has watched as his mother slowly became victim to dementia over the past five years. His father had died seven years ago and his mother took it badly. It was the start of a downward spiral in her mental health. When he could no longer be responsible for her safety Michael moved her into the care home but was sure to visit three times a week. The fact that David had invaded his mother's privacy so easily was enough for Michael to find a new home for his mother. He found a new home five miles further than the existing home. He arranged the immediate transfer of his mother and all her belongings. He didn't mind the extra travel if it meant his mother would be safe from David. Michael looks at his watch, his phone rings; he touches the screen of a tablet computer on his desk. He gets up and walks to Susan's office. He knocks and pushes his head round the door.

"They're here" Susan looks up, stops what she is doing and gets up. She follows Michael to the small meeting room. They sit at circular table. Shortly after Iris and Danny enter the room. Iris looks tired and drawn, Danny ushers Iris in first. Michael and Susan get up and offer their sympathies to Iris.

Michael "I am so sorry about Roger Iris that was no way for anyone to pass."

Iris shoots him a curt look "Fuck Roger, what the hell are we going to do about David? I spent over four hours with the police last night and avoided telling them about David fucking Todd."

Susan "I agree, we need to tell the police that David may be involved. They have the resources to find him and we need some kind of protection."

Danny, "Let's keep some perspective on this. If we run to the police they may start to dig into David's motives for what he's doing. Why he is doing this. That may not be in any of our best interests."

Iris, "Roger and Deepak are dead. We are next." She stares at Danny and continues "I'm for damn sure not going to be the next on his death list. I'm going to the police today and I suggest you all come with me. If we act together we can stop this bastard now. It's already too late for Roger and Deepak. I'm not listening to you anymore Danny. If anyone wants to come I'm going there at two o'clock." Iris gets up to go.

Michael "I have to visit my mother this morning. I need to check she's settled in, but I'll be back in time for two. I'll meet you at your office."

Susan "I'm in."

Danny "OK, we all meet at your office at two."

The visitors depart leaving Susan and Michael in the conference room.

`Susan "Give my love to Anne when you see her."

`Michael "I will. I'd better get going. I want to go over the new home one last time to make sure it has the appropriate security measures in place to prevent unwanted visitors. I still can't believe David managed to get so close to her. Makes my blood boil just thinking about it."

Susan "I can't imagine you angry Michael. I don't think I've ever seen you lose your temper in all the years that we've been partners."

Michael gets up and leaves the office "I'll see you later."

Danny exits the office building and hails a black cab. He gets in and calls Ian Draper

"Hi Ian, did you see her?" He asks without any pleasantries.

Ian "I saw her. She says she knows nothing and wants nothing to do with David. Definitely not a fan of yours and the others."

Danny "You believe her?"

Ian "I assume everyone is a liar. I've got a man watching her. You could be right. He may try to get in touch. Try to re-enter the life he knew."

Danny "We had a meeting. We're going to the police. You know what that means?"

Ian "I'm on it. I'll get everything in place."

Danny ends the call.

It had been a few days since Michael had visited Davina, his favourite escort. With all that had been going on and with the rising sense of anger within him he decided to spend a couple of hours with her before seeing his mother. Michael arranged to meet her at 10:30am, a bit earlier than usual, but it was going to be a busy day and he needed to relieve some tension.

Michael arrives at the Kensington address and parks on a bay. He pays by phone and heads to the Mansion block on the other side of the road. He pushes the intercom button for flat 6 and the main door clicks open. He enters. He gets to the door of flat 6 and wonders why he always feels a little nervous every time. He's been coming here for two years; surely he must be used to it? No, he always looks forward to seeing what she will wear to greet him. He wasn't disappointed. Davina opens the door wearing a big smile and a black latex dress with horizontal oval slits on both sides showing off her slim and toned body. Short black hair, five feet six and beautiful. Since leaving Uzbekistan four years ago she drifted into the escort business temporarily till she could find a permanent job. Davina found she had a skill for making men want what she had to offer and they were willing to pay a lot of money to enjoy those skills.

Davina "Michael, so good to see you my sweet," slight Russian accent making her seem even sexier to him.

Michael "These are for you," Michael hands Davina a bottle of wine and a small gift wrapped box.

Davina ushers Michael in and takes his coat "You take a seat and I'll get you a glass of wine."

Michael "It's a bit early, but I think I need one today." Michael goes to the living room and sits on the leather three seater. Davina follows him with a tray holding two glasses of red wine and the bottle.

`"Now my sweet Michael, what do you want me to do for you today?" Davina places the tray on the coffee table and sits next to Michael; she rubs her hand along his knee and up his thigh to his groin. "Come on, let's play a little game." She takes a sip of the wine then gets up and starts to dance seductively in front of Michael. As Davina gently moves her hips from side to side she unzips the dress slowly. She slips the straps off each shoulder and wriggles the dress to the floor. Davina is wearing a red micro thong and no bra. Michael watches as she slowly cups her incredible 34C breasts in her hands tempting him as she stares directly into his eyes. Michael takes in the vision in front of him. No matter how many times he has seen her naked he is always amazed by her sexiness. The perfect shape of her breasts, the smooth white skin, the toned body with that round firm arse. Davina is the perfect stripper, the perfect escort. Michael sits up on the edge of the sofa. He reaches up and gently takes hold of Davina's breasts. He fondles them enjoying the feel of her nipples growing against the palm of his hand as she becomes aroused. He knows how sensitive her nipples are. Davina lets out a sigh of pleasure as her breathing quickens. Michael goes on his knees kissing her firm flat stomach. He spins her around pushes her back onto the sofa slipping her thong down far enough to allow him access to her pussy. He lifts her legs in the air and positions his head between her legs. He licks her gently which sends a shiver of pleasure up her body. Encouraged by this reaction he continues darting his tongue in and out her pussy followed by short quick flicks on her clit. Michael rips off the thong which is still around her knees. He moves his attention to her breast as he licks and sucks at each nipple in turn. Davina is enjoying this. He always wondered whether she pretended or really was having fun.

Squeezing hers breast with both hands firmly he moves slowly down kissing her stomach as he approached her wet pussy. Michael buries his face in her pussy. He resumes his tongue assault on her. As he sucks on her clit he slips his middle finger into her gently rubbing her g-spot This drives her crazy, her breathing is heavy "Oh God, oh God" she repeats. Seeing her so excited has got him hard and ready. He straightens up and pulls off his shirt, and quickly undoes his belt and pulls his trousers and shorts down both at once. His stiff erect dick pops out. Davina grabs his hard eager penis. She slides off the sofa and with slick expertise slips a condom onto his penis as she slips it into her mouth. David knows what this means. Davina turns around and rests face down on the sofa. David moves in behind her still on his knees with his trousers around them. He shuffles closer to her wet tempting pussy. He places he penis into the wetness and pulls her towards him; he thrusts and feels the warmth of her pussy as he slides in all the way. Overwhelmed with excitement he starts to thrust hard, slowly at first then faster.

`"Come on you bitch, take it!" Michael closes his eyes as he shouts the words. "I'm gonna fuck you till you hurt." He slams hard against her repeatedly. He barely hears her plead with him to slow down.

"You're hurting me, please stop!" Davina tries to turn around, but Michael pushes her face down onto the sofa by the back of her neck, trapping her. He continues to fuck her harder and faster, ramming his cock in and out of her.

Michael opens his eyes, lost to whatever has possessed him. He grits his teeth and rasps the words "Fucking take it you bitch." He slaps her behind hard again and again leaving red streaks on that pert round white bottom. She squeals in pain as she struggles to get free of his grip on her neck. He grabs her hair and pulls her head back and up then places his left hand around her throat and starts to choke her. Scared and bewildered she tries to scream, but she can't. She opens her mouth and lunges to her left managing to reach his arm and bites it hard. He lets out a yell and shouts "You fucking whore!" He lets her go. She gets up quickly and runs to a small table in the corner of the room reaching into her handbag she grabs a small cylindrical device and presses a button.

In real fear she looks at Michael "You fucking crazy asshole! You get the fuck out of here!"

Michael "I'm not finished bitch, you gonna let me do what I want today" the pain in his arm fuelling his rage.

He gets up, pulls his trousers up and moves towards Davina. Before he can reach her he feels a sharp pain in his left side. Davina had pressed her panic alarm which summoned the large, well muscled Yuri from the spare room. The punch left Michael winded and agonised. He hit the floor hard landing on his knees. Yuri has a full on Russian accent mixed with a little South London "Get up you fuck" He reaches down and grabs Michael's hair pulling hard, forcing him onto his feet. Yuri is about to punch Michael in the face when he hears Davina's voice.

"No Yuri, just get him out of here. I don't want a dead asshole in my flat."

Yuri holds Michael by the back of this neck and shoves him through the room to the front door. Davina follows with Michael's shirt and coat hurling them at him.

"Get the fuck out. If I ever see you again I won't stop Yuri."

Michael stands stunned outside the flat. "What just happened?" he asks himself. He can't believe he completely lost control like that. He wanted to hurt, to punish that poor girl. Every fibre in his being was alive with a strange rage for a while. Ashamed and overwhelmed he limps down the stairs and out of the building. He tucks his shirt in and puts on his coat. Crosses the road to his car and set off still struggling to comprehend what happened.

Michael decides to go straight to the new care home. He arrives and pulls into the car park. He just wants to see his mother and get that relaxed comfortable feeling he always has in her presence. As he approaches the main door of the building he notices the door is ajar, unlocked. "Those bloody idiots" he feels the rage starting to grow again. He pushes the door. It swings open. Something's not right. There's no one behind the reception desk. No residents sitting on the sofas in reception no noise at all.

"Hey, where the hell is everyone?" He calls out. No response. Worried, he runs to the stairs and takes them two at a time, the pain in his arm and ribs gone replaced by fear for his mother's safety. He reaches the first floor and runs to his mother's room. He opens the door.

"Mum? Are you OK?" he asks as he enters. He sees her sitting in her easy chair by the window facing the door.

A voice comes from his right "Hello Michael," a chill washes over him. He looks around and sees David standing in the doorway of the en-suite.

Michael "You fucking bastard, leave her alone, she's done nothing to you."

David smiles and moves toward Anne "Not true. She gave birth to you. You are the product of her nurturing. She has to take some responsibility for your actions Michael."

Michael tries to move towards David. He can't. He wants so badly to squeeze David's throat, to crush his larynx, but he can't. He just stands there, frozen.

David "What's wrong Michael. You seem a little tense. How did your visit to your whore go? Did you fuck her brains out?"

Michael shoots a look at his mother.

David "Don't worry, she's hasn't a clue what's happening."

"What do you want?" Michael's voice masks his feeling of helpless. How is David holding him like this? Has he been drugged?

David "I'm glad you asked that question Michael. I propose we play a little game. I know you enjoy a good quiz so let's have one now. I going to ask you questions and you are going to answer. If I think you are telling the truth you will use one of the rather sharp surgical instruments to cut a part of your body off "David walks over to the bed and pulls aside a towel which was covering an assortment of scalpels, knives and syringes with needles.

"You're out of your fucking mind. Go to hell you sadistic bastard" Michael spits the words out.

"Let me finish, Michael. Where have your manners gone. Mummy must be so disappointed with the rude language being used" David tuts and continues "now if I think you're lying you are going to do something very unpleasant to mummy dear."

Michael's mind races "I called the police when I was downstairs, they'll be here any minute."

"Don't lie to me. You know what a lie means" David approaches Anne and stands behind her. "Hello Anne, It's me David, I gave you a card on your birthday, remember?"

Anne "Oh that's nice of you. Michael why are you just standing there? Get the nice man a cup of tea."

David "Oh, not for me dear; Michael and I are going to play a game and we want you to help" David strokes her hair gently.

Anne "That nice, Michael was always such a solitary boy. It's nice that he has someone to play with" Anne smiles.

David "Hear that Michael? Your mummy wants us to play."

Michael "Please David, I'll do anything you ask, just please leave her out of this."

Michael's words annoy David "Like you and the others left my family out of it when you all decided to fuck me over. Like that?" David sneers at him and rests a hand on Anne's shoulder. "My wife and children suffered every step of the way while you and the others quietly trousered tens of millions each. I don't recall you demonstrating any remorse for them then, which is why I thought perhaps a lesson in empathy would help you grow as a human being. Don't you agree Anne?"

Anne "What's that dear?"

David ignores her response. He just wants to get on with the game.

David "Anne told me you wet the bed till you were eleven Michael, is that true?"

Anne "It is true, remember Michael; I can still smell your bedroom. We went through so many mattresses."

Michael looks at his mother "Shut up mother!" he shouts, anger in him stirring as bad memories come flooding back.

David "That's no way to talk to your mother Michael, what else did he do Anne? I want to hear all his embarrassing little secrets."

Anne "Well dear, I caught him once when he was older playing in his bedroom with little Timmy."

Michael's fuming now and still unable to move "Shut up you senile old bitch!"

Anne "There he was little Timmy; Timmy was what we called his penis by the way, anyway little Timmy in hand eyes shut and he was quite in his own world. I didn't have the heart to stop him so I just waited."

Michael's face is contorted with rage "Shut up you crazy fucking bitch!" he shouts.

David "Who's idea was it to set me up?"

Michael still in a fit of rage looks at David "Go fuck yourself; I don't know what the hell you're talking about." Michael stops talking. He realises what he has just said.

David "Now that is a lie. You must really hate mummy dear right now. Keep talking Anne. I want to know all Michael's little secrets" Anne continues to talk. David looks at Michael "Michael, you know the rules. You lied, now mummy must suffer. I want you to pick up a scalpel and slowly slice off your mother's left ear. Do it now."Michael feels compelled to walk to the bed. He lumbers toward the bed trying hard, but unable to resist; he just keeps moving.

Michael begs "Please David, I don't know how you're doing this, but please stop it," Michael hears yet another embarrassing story from his early teen coming from his mother's mouth. He is dizzy from memories he had long since forgotten. His rage at David building, rage at his mother and her fucking stories growing. The fear of what he was about to do tempers his rage slightly. He reaches the bed and picks up a scalpel, turns around and takes a step towards Anne. David takes up position behind Anne, quietly watching, savouring every moment. Michael reaches his mother. She is still reeling off tales from his past. A story about how he shit himself at school during PE. Why can't she just shut up? Michael stands directly in front of his mother looking at her. She looks up at him

"Hello dear, I was just talking about you."

David "Cut now."

Michael's arm shakes as he struggles to break the control over him. His eyes stream with tears "I'm so sorry mummy." He lowers the scalpel onto his mother's left ear. He slowly draws the sharp blade back slicing easily half an inch downwards. Blood oozes out running down to her neck. Anne screams in agony. She grabs Michael by the waist. Michael slices forward cutting almost a full inch now. All he can see is a bloody mess. Anne screams again. Hugging onto Michael she looks up at him eyes filled will tears and terror.

"Please stop Michael, please!" Anne pleads. Michael draws the blade back once more and the ear just gives way as the blade finishes its journey. The ear falls to the floor. Michael stands motionless. Blood dripping from the blade he is still holding. His mother weeps in pain, bewildered by her son's behaviour.

David "Wow; that was intense. Now, do I need to repeat the question? I may have to speak up for mummy dear to hear now" David chuckles at his own sick joke. Michael stares at the ear on the floor. He wants so badly to stick the blade into David's chest. He is standing just a couple of feet in front of him and yet he may as well be fifty feet from him.

David "Who's idea was it?"

Michael knows David knows the answer. This game will not end well for him or his mother. Its better that he be truthful and suffer than have her take any more pain. Her heart is sure to give out. He looks at her still bleeding from the wound he inflicted.

Michael "Danny. It was Danny's idea."

David "At last. A correct answer. You know what that means?"

Michaels hears the words, but can't believe it. David repeats "I want you to cut off your left eyelid" his voice calm and tempered. David observes Michael's reaction. Michael looks up at David. Excitement etched on his face. He is really enjoying this. Michael slowly reaches up with his left hand, pulls his left eyelid forward. He positions the scalpel above and to the left of his now protruding eyelid. He pulls the scalpel across in one motion. He screams as blood leaks onto his unprotected eyeball.

Michael "You fucking bastard!" he shouts at David.

David whoops with amazement "Wow! This is incredible. Now, next question. Did you and Susan falsify the due diligence or was it just you?"

Michael's hands shake; the mental and physical stress telling on him.

"Both of us" he answers. He wants to wipe the blood dripping onto his exposed eyeball but can't.

David "See how easy this is. Now I want you to cut off your left index finger. No, change my mind. Too simple for you. I know you prefer a challenge after all it must have been a complex tasks to falsify those financials for Genova. Presenting a new set of accounts which were miraculously discovered at the last minute and somehow validated must have been very difficult to pull off. A simple cut is too easy. I want you to fillet your left index finger."

Michael "Go fuck yourself. I'm not doing it" Michael is defiant but his body obeys. He holds out his left hand palm up. He pierces the skin at the base of his index finger. Blood seeps out. He whimpers then yells as he cuts along the length of his finger up to the sensitive tip. Breathing heavily and trembling all over he drops the scalpel as he proceeds to peel the skin and flesh from the bone. Slowly he separates the bone from sinews and connective tissue. His eyes roll up and back in pain.

David warns him "Don't faint now, or it's just me and mummy dear" not even sure Michael can hear him. David watches as Michael peels the finger back to the base leaving the bloodied bone exposed. He knows that Michael won't be able to take much more.

David "Fuck me that was special."

Anne suddenly chirps up "He's a fucking idiot."
Both men look at her.

"You heard me. You fucking idiot. I can't believe I gave birth to such a weak pathetic man. You were weak as a child now you are a weak man. You're a waste of space you piece of shit. No wonder you couldn't find a woman, who would want you?"

Michael "Please stop, stop it!" how could this woman who doted on him all his life say these things. "Stop making her say these things" he shouts at David.

David laughs and shakes his head, "Not me, all her."

Anne "Why couldn't you leave home like other boys?"

Michael's rage returns. He feels betrayed by his own mother "Shut up bitch or I'll cut your other ear off" he yells.

David "No, we've done that already, just do something different. You know, mix it up"

Michael's rage turns to fury. He screams at his mother "Shut up! Stop it now!" he rushes over to her. She continues to shout abuse at him. His teeth bared and almost snarling he attempts to cover her mouth with his damaged hand. The skin and flesh slapping at her face. She shakes her head back and forth.

Anne "Fuck off you idiot" he slaps her with his right hand. That felt good. He slaps her again hitting the cavity where her ear was. With each slap the fury builds then the slaps turns to punches. He punches her with his left hand. His exposed index finger bones dig into her face. His right fist smashes into her nose breaking it. He continues the onslaught. His fists raining down damaging blow after blow. His index finger bone breaks off and drops to the ground. Consumed with hatred and anger he feels no more pain.

"Your fucking fault, your fucking fault" he repeats with each blow till his arms tire. Exhausted he stops and sinks to his knees. He looks up at his mother's face. "Oh God, what have I done?" her face is beaten to a pulp. The bone structure battered to an unrecognisable mush of blood, flesh and bone. He looks at his fists aware of a growing pain. His hands are broken and gashed from the bones in his mother's face.

David "Well, well Michael just one more thing and we are done."

Michael is completely broken.

David "I want Danny's access information for the accounts in Dubai and Singapore." Michael mumbles. David moves closer, putting his ear to Michael's mouth. Michael whispers the information to him. David takes out a small pad and pen and makes notes.

David "I guess the games over. Not quite what I expected, but hugely enjoyable. Now Michael, you have a choice. On the bed is a syringe filled with concentrated sulphuric acid. You can either inject this into your chest or beat your head against the wall over there till your brains fall out." Michael struggles to his feet and walks to the bed. He tries to pick up the syringe with his broken hands. With agonising pain he manages to lift the syringe to his chest using both hands he positions the long needle against his sternum. The pain in his hands is unbearable. The syringe slips, but he manages to steady it. He now just wants the pain to go. He focuses and pulls the syringe hard towards his chest, puncturing the sternum and sinking the needle into his heart, he flushes the toxic liquid into his body. The effect is immediate and violent. He thrashes around as blood spurts from his mouth and nose. His eyeballs redden then pop, bloody liquid oozes out. Michael falls to the floor still convulsing as life slowly leaves his body.

David smiles and leaves the room. He arrives at his flat, goes to the bedroom and pulls the box from under the bed. He looks at Shithead.

David "Your whole arm is gone now. Three more."

Shithead opens its mouth. He's hungry. David puts a bit of a sandwich in the open slit. The creature eats greedily, and then it sticks its tongue out asking for lager.

7 Reasons and Motives

Detective Inspector Jennifer James surveys the mess in Anne's room. In all her twelve years as a police woman she has never seen a crime scene so violent and sadistic. She hears a commotion at the door of the room and turns to look. It's Susan; she is Michael's emergency contact in the event of a problem.

DI James is thirty seven and entered the Police force as a trainee constable then progressed onto the Detective route. Five feet six tall; a little on the portly side and always dresses in ladies trousers and jacket when working. She wears no makeup and has shoulder length brown hair tied up in a pony tail. "Who are you?"

Susan "I'm Susan Chang, Michael Howard's business Partner. What's happened? Is Anne OK?" She asks the questions not expecting a reassuring answer.

DI James looks at the officer at the door "Let her in." She looks at Susan and continues "You will find this distressing Miss Chang, are you sure you want to see this?"

Susan's voice is tearful and scared "I have to."

The smell hits her first; a strange mix of some sort of chemical and faeces or rotting organic material. She sees Anne's body still propped up in the easy chair. She bursts into tears and gags at the same time, both appalled and revolted. As she staggers back a policeman steadies her. Susan then glimpses the remains of Michael. His body contorted from the agonising painful death from within. Acidic foam still slowly seeping from his mouth onto the floor in an effervescent puddle. The smell of shit emanating from him as the acid burnt its way through his alimentary canal. It's too much for Susan. As she faints the policeman catches her.

Susan regains consciousness and slowly comes to.

"Susan, are you OK?" she hears Danny's voice.

Susan's eyes open fully as she remembers everything. Danny is kneeling beside her as she lies on a sofa in the reception area of the complex. Danny hugs her and she starts to cry again. The complex is under lock down and all the residents have been asked to stay in their rooms.

She looks into Danny's eyes "Its David. He's killed them both. He's going to kill us all Danny, we have to get away from here."

DI James "About this David Todd Miss Chang, we have taken statements from Mr Havers and Mrs Caldwell. If you are up to it we'd like to take a statement from you too."

Susan sits up "A statement? OK. His name is David Todd. He's out there killing my friends because he blames us for something that happened over four years ago. You won't find him because he doesn't live at an address, he is a vagrant and he is killing us one by one."

DI James "I assure you Miss Chang if there is something to what you say, homeless or not we will find him, but currently looking at the facts all indications point to the previous deaths being suicide and even this scene looks very much like Mr Howard beat his mother to death then took his own life; albeit in a very bizarre manner. Now were it not for the fact that all the victims are linked to yourselves and acid was used I may have been inclined to count this as a murder suicide, however it does look like Mr Howard's death was designed to be very brutal and painful."

Iris has been sitting quietly, stunned by the brutality of the deaths and now further scared about her own fate "How the hell did he manage to knock out all these people? There were over twelve staff and twenty residents," Iris asks not sure whether she wants to hear the answer. She looks at Danny as he comforts Susan, envious and wanting to feel his arms around her. Danny glance's at Iris as if to say "It's you I'd rather be hugging."

DI James "We don't know yet, but the Forensics team are on it. We are communicating with the other officers from the previous scenes. It's just a question of time before the media get their teeth into this, so it may serve our purpose to call them now if we have good reason to believe Mr Todd may be behind all of this," she looks at Iris and continues, "now, if we had a motive with some proof that would be a start. Why does he want you dead?" she is blunt. The question is simple and she observes the reaction of the group closely. They are all on edge, but they are sticking together. Clearly they are hiding something.

DI James "If you want our help then you will have to give us something to understand why this man may be doing this," Danny looks at Iris as he squeezes Susan's arm.

The unsaid message is "Say nothing."

DI James knows if she is to get anyone to talk she will have to speak to them separately. Her mobile phone bursts into a chorus of Barry Manilow's Copacabana. She takes the phone out of her trouser pocket and turns round to answer it. She walks off as she speaks to the caller.

Iris looks at Danny "We have no choice. We have to tell them. We act now and the police can inform the media today."

Danny looks to ensure no one is in earshot "Bullshit Iris, they start to look into this and we stand to lose everything. I don't know how David is doing this, but we outsmarted him once, we can do it again."

Iris "We didn't outsmart him you ass, we ambushed him. He trusted us and we fucked him, now he is the one doing the fucking. This is not some corporate game Danny, my husband and two friends have been brutally murdered and that maniac is still out there with us in his sights."

Susan has been desperately fighting the desire to scream and run out of this place. She looks up at Danny "Iris is right. We need their help." She knows Danny. He won't listen. His ego won't allow it, to think that David has them against the ropes. No, him running scared? Even if the truth is staring them in the face in the form of five grisly corpses. No.

Danny checks to ensure the DI is still on the phone "OK, look, I've got Ian out there with a team of people looking for David. If by 5pm today he hasn't found him then I will give the police enough for them to go to the media. I need to let the Board know first. If this comes out without any damage control the company's stock will take a serious hit, and we may all be out of a job. Now I don't know about you, but I'm pretty sure that it's going to be hard to find another job in the square with the money and benefits we are enjoying, especially if we have a shadow on us. I suggest we..."

Before he can finish DI James returns "Well, it looks like we are making progress."

They all look at her not sure whether they want to hear what she has to say.

DI James smiles slightly "Looks like we have motive" Danny flinches, tightening his hold on Susan.

DI James continues "Theft, pure and simple theft. Well maybe not so simple. Both Mr Patel and Mr Caldwell appear to have transferred large amounts of money from their UK accounts to accounts in Dubai and Singapore. You people get paid a lot."

Susan sees a glimmer of hope "You should be able to get the Dubai account information, but some Singapore banks still don't like to share."

DI James "We have people working on it, but it may take some time. The funds may have been bounced from account to account in different countries."

Susan feeling a little more in control now "Banking is what we do, why don't you let us help you. Give me the details you need checked and we can use the banks resources to speed things up." She stands up and approaches the policewoman "What will take you days will take us hours. Please, I don't want to end up like the others."

DI James "Under the circumstances I don't think involving any of you will be possible. At the moment we can't rule out anyone from our enquiries."

Susan incredulous "What? You think we may be involved in this?"

DI James "It's been a long difficult week for all of you. I suggest that you all go home for now till we get the forensics back. I'll be in touch with each of you." The group look at each other.

Danny speaks "No, not home. We need to get back to work. I've had Ashton's pit-bull on the phone every ten minutes wanting an update on the Mantech deal."

Iris looks at Danny "Surely you don't think we can possibly continue without Michael and Roger?"

Danny, "We can't just turn our backs on the company. We need to finish this takeover. I have final drafts from Michael, and you Iris can complete Roger's work. Come on, you've been doing it for years."

DI James "Please let us know where you will be and if possible make sure you check on each other. Now if you'll excuse me I have to oversee clearing this mess up."

Danny, Susan and Iris head back to work. DI James watches as the three leave and wonders what these people could have done to someone which would warrant such violence. Time to find out a little more about Mr Todd.

Mary liked to get away from her desk for lunch. Stale piss smelling firm partner John Langley was forever asking her to have lunch in some greasy spoon which he swore made THE best deep fried pork belly sandwich. Just the thought was enough to engage her gag reflex. Mary secured the job with the small firm of Solicitors in Tooting, South London a couple of years ago. It was perfect for her to travel to and from Clapham by public transport or car and within easy reach of the children's' school. She usually drove to the nearby station, parked and jumped on the underground. The area was always alive and bustling with a vibrant primarily Asian community occupying much of the high street. Today she wanted to sit in a little cafe just off the high street and enjoy a grilled cheese and tomato sandwich washed down with a latte.

These past few days she hadn't been able to stop thinking about her ex-husband. She wasn't missing him, no, all those feelings had long gone and been replaced with resentment and loathing. After it all went wrong she had stuck by him. The money and the "things" didn't matter. She had tried time and time again to get him to move on. Get him to stop the drinking and obsessing trying to work out what went wrong. She would hear him from the bedroom as he sat in the living room, pacing and talking to himself. She could swear that there were times he would change his voice and talk back to himself. He deteriorated very quickly. From a man who barely drank alcohol to monster with an unquenchable thirst for the stuff in a matter of weeks. She had feared for the children and herself, then one day she came home and he was gone. He had walked, danced or whatever the hell out of the house leaving her to deal with the mess of all the bills and debts. She took what free advice was available, sold off everything of value and put the house up for sale, cheap.

Four years later she's at the point where she and the children are in a comfortable routine. Money is always very tight which means they go without a lot, but she has control of her life. That was until Ian Draper showed up at her door asking about David. She could not imagine the man she married could do any of the things Mr Draper spoke of, but it has been four years and his mental state was not good when he left. Perhaps he is responsible. Mary dismissed the thoughts "To hell with them." She will not let this become her problem, not now, not after all the heartache and hardship.

"Fuck them all" she whispers to herself and approaches the lights to cross the road. These lights always took forever to change. The button was already pressed so it could change soon. Mary looked at the other side of the road. There looking at her was Ian Draper. That bastard was following her. He just stood there opposite waiting to cross, just staring at her in a very odd way. A lorry speeds past briefly blocking him out, but as it passes he is still there. She wanted to rush over to him and shout "Leave me alone!"

Cars, vans and buses rush past. Mary and Ian staring at each other. The lights still in favour of the relentless traffic. Suddenly Ian takes a step forward. Mary looks at the signal again, the red man still showing. Ian takes another step forward; she looks to her left and right, a white van moving swiftly coming from her right. She looks back at Ian. He keeps walking towards her. He must have seen the van, she's sure. He's just trying to time his crossing, but as she looks at him he just stares at her as if transfixed. An old Indian man on the other side shouts at Ian "watch out man!" Ian stops in the middle of the road. Everyone watching relieved as the van approaches blaring its horn. The driver sees him stop and continues forward without braking. Mary watches Ian with a strange fascination. Something is wrong, his face soaked in sweat mouthing something. It looks like "Help me," before she can see anymore Ian takes a step forward, the van slams into him sending him flying, the sound of the impact almost covered by the sound of screeching tyres as the driver hits the brake. There are screams and gasps as witnesses appalled and horrified by what has happened recover their senses and rush over to the still bundle of bones, skin and flesh lying about fifteen feet from the front of the van. Mary covers her face with her hands as she hears a man voice to her left exclaim "Fuck me! Did you see that!?" A familiar voice. Mary spins to her left. There right beside her is David looking at the gathering crowd.

Mary, voice trembling and face now with tears running down "Did you do this?" she asks afraid of the answer. David feigns surprise at the question as he points to himself

"Moi? I just saw you as I was coming out of the Chicken Cottage over there and came over to surprise you."

Mary, angry now "Don't fuck with me David, did you do this?"

David, calmly and slowly "Mary, I did not do this, but you'd expect a Private Eye to have better peripheral vision" he chuckles to himself internally. "Look let me buy you a coffee."

Mary "I need something stronger" she points to a pub, "Over there."

David returns to the table with large gin and tonic and an orange juice.

David "Here you go, that should stop the shaking. Ironically without it I shake like a washing machine on spin." Mary takes the gin and gulps half of it in one. David looks around the old traditional style pub. Not many like these left in this area. Give it another year before it becomes a restaurant. The landlord was clearly trying to make the place festive in the hope of attracting back customers lost to the new Wine Bar across the road and the several new coffee shops that had sprung up in the last couple of years. She takes a big sip of the drink and puts the glass down

"Do you expect me to believe that you just happen to show up as that man walks in front of a van?" she is visibly still shaken by the road incident.

David "I don't give a shit what you believe, I was nowhere near that man and there are plenty of witnesses including yourself." Mary thinks for a moment. There was no way he could have been responsible. He was right beside her at the time. She examines David. He's older, thinner and somehow seems smaller. It's an expensive suit, shoes, watch the works.

Mary "What do you want?"

David "I want to help you."

Mary "I needed your help four years ago. Now I just need you to stay out of my life."

David leans forward "How are the kids?"

Mary "That's none of your business."

David "Come on Mary, they're my children too. I have a right to know" the second he finished the sentence he knew he had pushed a button; Mary leans forward and snarls as the words come out "You don't have any rights. You fucked off one day and left us. You have no fucking rights you piece of shit."

David "Wow. Your vocabulary has certainly expanded. I know what I did was wrong. I'm not asking for forgiveness or second chances just to help you with a bit of money and in return you let me see the kids for an hour or so."

Mary is appalled "You want me to sell you time with my children? The same children who cried themselves to sleep for months after you went walkabout? The same children who have now moved on to the point where you are just a faint memory at certain times of the year. No David. The answer is no now and forever."

David sits back "No, no, I'm not trying to buy time with them just an opportunity to see them and at the same time help you out." Mary doesn't even have to think,

"No. Now I have to get back to work" she downs the rest of the drink and moves to get up. David rests his left hand on her right shoulder to stop her and perhaps to give him an excuse to touch her "Wait, please. Mary, I've changed. I'm getting my life back together. I've got a place to stay and some money now. Maybe I can see you again later this week?"

Mary sits "David, people you used to call your friends are dying and for some reason they believe you are to blame. Are you?"

David shakes his head "I swear Mary, I've not laid a finger on any of them. Those so called friends stabbed me in the back and destroyed my entire life" he pauses and continues "Our lives."

Mary sighs, leans forward and looks David in the eyes "I don't care. The children and I are happy again. It's strange, up to just a few weeks ago I was worried sick every day wondering how to make ends meet, how to afford things for the children, just about everything. Then one day I woke up and everything just seemed so peaceful. Like all was going to be fine. I truly believe that we are happy now. I used to pray every day for help to get to the other side of this river we had been pushed into. Now we are climbing out of that damn river you and your friends or enemies pushed us into I'll be damned if I'll let you drag us back in."

David "You don't understand. They used bribery and false accounting to sabotage the vote to prevent the licensing for the chip Genova had developed. They made tens of millions each and set themselves up in the company I brought them into whilst I was left to rot" David is getting angry. He composes himself aware that Mary is scrutinising him.

She gets up and grabs her handbag "I want nothing to do with you. Stay away from us" she walks out of the pub.

For the rest of the afternoon Mary could not concentrate on her work. Several mistakes later she suddenly felt a little queasy. When she left the pub there were still policemen taking statements from onlookers at the scene of Draper's "accident". The more she thought about it the more she remembered his eyes staring at her, as if pleading for help. He must have seen that van coming. Why would he just step out in front of it like that? Mary can't focus on her work. She had told her boss about the incident and he had insisted that she take the afternoon off to compose herself. She had declined the offer, but now with all that had happened, and with the silly mistakes she is making she decides to take her boss' offer up and sets off home.

Mary reaches the small three bedroom terrace house the council had placed her and the children in. She had agonised over applying for the house, but her father made her see sense, with all of the money they had lost defending legal action and what shares David had accumulated driven so low by the adverse publicity the company received after David's take over deal went sour she had no choice. She didn't wanted to rely on her father for money, after all it was him who warned her to find a nice Jewish boy, but for the first two years he had helped to support them and insisted she prayed each and every day until it became a ritual for her.

As Mary opens the gate to the tiny front garden she hears her name being called from behind her "Hi, are you Mary Todd?" Mary turns to see a woman and a man and woman approaching her "Sorry to startle you. I'm Detective Inspector James and this is my colleague DI Blaine" they lift up their ID as they reach Mary.

DI Blaine is about five feet eight and quite thin. He is forty five and has been a Detective for ten years. His progress up the ranks stalled seven years ago and he is content to remain in his current role. Although he is wearing a suit it looks like he may have slept in it "We just have a few questions we'd like to ask you about your ex-husband" Mary looks around the street.

Mary "King, Its Mary King now. You'd better come in."

Mary opens the door and the officers follow her into the house. The hallway is small as you would expect from the size of the frontage. This is not the best part of Clapham, but for Mary it is the most affordable and recently the prices had been going up and she hoped to one day get the right to buy the property at a huge discount. The hallway walls are papered with floral wallpaper which looks like it's been hung since the nineteen seventies. The floor is covered in a grey hardwearing carpet, the kind you find in cheap hotel rooms. Mary shows the officers into the living/dining room. This room continues the theme of minimalism and the seventies. Same carpet as the hallway, but the walls are painted white. At least they used to be. There is a square glass dining table with four wooden chairs at the rear of the room and a three seater sofa at the other end against the wall adjoining the hallway. A small flat screen television sits on a table opposite the sofa. Mary gestures to the officers to take a seat at the dining table as she switches the light on.

DI James takes out her pad and pen "Thank you for seeing us. It's about your ex-husband Ms King. There have been some quite horrific incidents involving Mr Todd's ex colleagues in the last week," she looks at Mary observing her reactions.

Mary looks at the officers then settles her gaze on DI James "I've heard about the deaths, and to be frank I don't give a rat's arse about any of them."

DI James looks at her colleague with a puzzled expression "We've not released any information to the public, how did you find out?"

Mary "Well, their pet dog Mr Draper has been calling and I met David today"

DI Blaine shoots a startled look at Mary "What! Where did you meet?"

Mary remembers the incident and pauses to collect her thoughts before continuing "It was on Tooting High Street and Mr Draper was there across the road. Then he just stepped out in front of a van."

DI Blaine "Who? Mr Todd?"

Mary "No, Mr Draper, he just stared at me and walked in front of a van. He's dead."

DI James "Walked or was pushed? Where was Mr Todd?"

Mary "He was standing just behind me. He couldn't have pushed him then get to where he was, not possible."

DI Blaine gets his phone out and walks to the hallway.

DI James "Are you OK Ms King? Do you need a hot drink or some water?"

Mary shakes her head "I haven't seen him in four years and the minute he shows up that man dies in front of me."

DI James "What did he say to you?"

Mary "He said he hadn't laid a single finger on any of them. He also said he wasn't drinking any more, but he reeked of booze so I really don't know what to believe."

DI Blaine returns and takes his seat again. He looks at his partner "She's right. There was an incident at lunch time which resulted in Mr Draper being struck by a van. There were several witnesses who confirm he just stepped out onto the road and walked into the oncoming vehicle. The driver is still in shock."

DI James "Bodies are piling up Ms King; we need to know where your ex-husband is staying."

Mary "He said he was staying with a friend. He didn't look like he was living rough, even had on a clean suit."

DI Blaine "Where Ms King, where is he ?"

Mary "He didn't say, I didn't ask. I was still shock. I'd just seen a man killed. I'm sorry; I just didn't think to ask."

DI James puts her right hand on Mary's left hand "It's OK love, take it easy, anything you can remember can be useful. Did he say what he was doing in the area?"

Mary pulling her hand away "Yes, he wanted to give me money in return for spending time with the kids. I said no and told him to stay away from us and left."

DI James "How much money? Did he say where he got this money from?"

Mary "No, I refused. He didn't go into details about the money."

DI Blaine "Did he give you a contact number, anything?"

Mary getting angry now "I said no! Don't you think I would give you any information if I had any?"

DI James "What was his mood like? Did he seem normal?"

Mary shakes her head slightly "David hasn't been normal for a long time. For months after we lost everything he hit the bottle hard. I could hear him downstairs in the old house, drinking and talking to himself; all hours of the night and day. He'd just lock himself away in that study and I have to say it scared us all. There were times when I thought there was someone else in there with him, but I think he had some sort of psychotic break. He was just talking to himself."

DI Blaine "How did he end up on the streets?"

Mary "I came home one day in October four years ago and he was gone, till today."

DI Blaine "What about his friends and family?"

Mary "He was an only child and both his parents died years ago. As for friends, I think you've met the only friends he had. David was about the work and the money. When all that was taken away from him he just fell apart. No, no friends."

DI James "Any ideas where he might be. Does he have any favourite places to visit?"

Mary "Just drive around the square mile and you'll probably see him. He was always married more to the City than he was to me." Mary looks at her watch "I don't mean to be rude but the kids will be home soon and I need to get some cooking done." The officers stand up and walk to the hallway. Mary opens the door and they step out. DI James turns to Mary and hands her a card "This is my number. If you hear from him again or remember anything else please get in touch." Mary takes the card and closes the door. She walks back to the living room and slumps onto the sofa.

As the officers walk back to their car DI Blaine's phone rings. He answers it listening for a few seconds then "Really? That's interesting. OK Jan, thanks for that." He ends the call and looks at DI James "They've traced the first bank transfers to destination. You're gonna find this interesting."

8 The Show Must Go On

David is sitting on the single bed in his new almost City basement flat. He pulls the shoebox from under the bed eager to see what part of Shithead has disappeared post Ian Draper's exit to the other side. As he pulls back the handkerchief used to cover Shithead he wonders why Draper's death was so much less interesting than the others.

David is disappointed "No change little fella. I don't understand. I saw him die just a couple of hours ago. Did you or didn't you kill that bastard?" The creature stirs, shifting its bulb like body in a bid to display its pleasure at the news and to express another desire for some of the tasty liquid that David has been feeding it. David knows immediately what to do and pours a little Stella from a tin into the slit of a mouth. Satisfied, Shithead whispers something to David. He moves closer to hear. David pulls back "Not you? Then why would he just walk out like that. Never seemed the suicidal type. Yeah you're right, fuck him." David realises he didn't have to lean forward to hear Shithead when it said "fuck him" the voice just seemed to be in his head. Same whispering hiss of a voice, but in his head.

David "Did you just say, fuck him?"

The voice in his head answers again "That right, we still have the others to deal with. Now feed me." David puts the creature down and walks to the hallway and picks up a KFC box. He wonders, as he often does, whether he has lost his fucking mind, and is about to feed an empty shoebox for the hundredth time. He has considered taking a photo of Shithead and showing it to the man at the offie to see his reaction. He could say "What the fuck man, it's an empty box, or, "What the fuck is that man, some weird doll you freak?" Either way he would know whether he was bonkers or had truly spawned a new species of bottom dwelling creature. Neither conclusion was comfortable to think about. All David knew was that when Shithead appeared, as painful as it was, everything got better. He returns to the bedroom and sets about feeding Shithead chicken and chips.

After twenty minutes of feeding Shithead speaks in his head again "Susan is next to be punished."

David sheepishly responds "You know, I was thinking about Susan, does she have to, you know?"

Shithead "All six must die."

David "I know, but she was always good to me, we even kissed once at a Christmas party."

Shithead "All six will die" the voice seemed a little louder this time.

David "Can't we just scare her to within millimetres of her life?"

Suddenly the voice is thunderous and booming "ALL SIX WILL DIE. ALL SIX WILL DIE. ALL SIX WILL DIE..." over and over the voice beams its message directly into David's head, piercing and invasive as it delivers a stunning blow each time; David falls to his knees, the pain from the voice too much to bear,

"OK! OK! I'm sorry. She must die."

The assault stops instantly. David breathless and still disorientated manages to get back onto the bed. About a minute of silence passes then Shithead speaks in his normal hiss "You want to fuck her?" it asks tauntingly.

David "No, I don't want to have sex with her."

Shithead "Do you want to fuck her? I will allow it if you want."

David raises his voice now "No! I don't want to fuck her!"

The creature persists; seeming to be enjoying the exchange "You can fuck her before we kill her or maybe while we're killing her" it pauses then "How about after we kill her?"

David appalled and disgusted "Fuck you! That's just sick you fucking piece of shit!"

All David hears is "Heh, heh, heh" then Shithead says something they can both agree on "I'm thirsty" David picks up the shoebox and pours some Stella into the thing's mouth, he then gets up and walks to the kitchen and opens a bottle of Jack.

The board room at AKM Investment Bank, Danny is sitting at the twenty one seater board table. At the head of the table is the CEO, Ashton Carter, a sixty two year old banker with forty years experience in banking. Twelve of those forty years as CEO of AKM. A tall thin man with a strong chin and eyes which look at you with suspicion always. He is completely bald and even at his age has no need for spectacles. He is wearing a tailored pinstripe suit which says nothing more than "Banker." He is not dressed to impress, merely has the demeanour of a man who needs not to wear the hundreds of millions he has accumulated over the years about his person. To his right is his CFO, Reg Copeland, and to his left head of his head of legal Alan Dick. The CFO is a small man who started in the company as an accountant and rose through the ranks. Short cut side parted hair; fifteen stones, which on a short frame makes him look uncomfortably overweight. Dressed in a grey Boss suit he has over the years tried to dress the part of a City Executive. He didn't have to bother, his grasp of the rules and regulations of Corporation tax in the UK and abroad and his ability to find tax avoidance loopholes for the benefit of the company has proven immensely valuable.

Mr Dick looks every part a corporate Lawyer. A tailored well fitting suit surrounds his taught thirty five year old body. Though young, he has also proven his worth repeatedly in the past in interpreting Legislations and getting the company out of tight spots that would otherwise have cost the company a small fortune. Full head of brushed back hair, he has always reminded Danny of the Gordon Gekko character in the movie. Mr Dick's only problem in life was his name. He has gone through life with the name A Dick. He could have changed it, but that ridiculous name has spurred him on to achieve a top post in a major Investment Bank with an eye watering remuneration package at a very early age.

Ashton, Alan and Reg look at Danny with some discontent. A troubled Ashton wants answers from Danny "What the fuck is going on Danny? We've got three dead employees and a dead external asset."

Danny shifts uncomfortably in his chair. He has never been on the receiving end of this sort of meeting before. He holds Ashton's look "This may be a little hard to believe, but I think David is behind the killings."

Ashton looks puzzled "David? David fucking who?" he asks knowing what the answer will be.

Danny reluctantly "You know, David Todd..." he holds Ashton's stare expecting the penny to drop and it does.

Ashton mockingly "Oh, that David, the one who you replaced and have been keeping an eye on since he opted to coexist with London's degenerates. The last report I had from you saw him fully ensconced in a doorway every night about twenty minutes from here. Your report said he was not to be a threat to this firm ever again. That fucking David?"

Danny shifts in his seat again "I don't know how, but I am certain he is behind these killings. We've all seen him, albeit briefly, but I think he's been following us."

Ashton "Why? He fucked up the takeover, why would he want to massacre your team. On that point, I've spoken with the police and the evidence so far points to two suicides and one murder suicide. Not sure what the hell happened to Draper, but he was external so who gives a shit. My point is why? Do you know something I don't Danny?"

Danny gives Ashton his best I'm being sincere look "No Ashton, maybe he just cracked, or took some bad drugs, I really don't know, but we've got to get the police to put his name and face out there."

Ashton looks at the men to his left and right then shakes his head "No, no, no that is the last thing we are going to do. We are going to let the police do their work. They have David's details I presume?"

Danny "Yes."

Ashton "Great, then all we need do is go about our business as usual. Have security arrange for bodyguards for you and what's left of your team today. The takeover agreement for Mantech is ready, so let's just make some money."

Danny "But Ashton, this man is managing to do things that are incredible. He seems able to get past building security completely undetected."

Ashton looks at Danny and lets out a deep sigh "You know something Danny. When David was in charge he minted money. Deal after deal, I would get a hard on every day just watching the company stock price rise. Every day I'd go home and fuck the brains out of my lovely young wife. I'd fuck her in the bedroom, fuck her in the bathroom, fuck her in the kitchen, everywhere. Now, since you've been in charge I get the odd tingling sensation but no hard on. You know what that means Danny?"

Danny shakes his head "No."

Ashton "Means I can't fuck my lovely young wife with the customary vigour. She used to be unable to get out of bed the next morning let alone walk, now she bounces out of bed every morning at 6 am like a fucking gazelle on speed. Then she goes to the gym, has lunch with the other lovely young wives and then you know what she does? She goes shopping Danny. This week she had a life size statue of her father made and stuck it in the fucking driveway. I wouldn't mind, but the man is still alive. She bought seven swans. I don't even know where you buy swans from but she did. Seven swans Danny, seven fully fucking grown swans walking all over my impeccably manicured lawns, shitting and pecking, but not one has shit on the statue yet. You get my drift Danny?" Danny nods.

Ashton "No hard on, no vigorous fucking and an out of control lovely young wife. All these things you are going to fix by Christmas. OK?"

Danny "Sure Ashton, I just want to reassure you I can get on top of this."

Ashton "Excellent Danny, for a minute there you looked like a man treading water with a dumbbell tied to your testicles. Your face was saying one thing but underneath you looked like you were in pain. Didn't he look like that?" Ashton looks at the two men either side of him. They both nod in agreement.

Reg looks up and poses a question "What about Patel Ash?"

Ashton looks at Reg "What about him?"

Reg "Well he's all over the net. If the media manage to tie that in with what else has been going on around here then we could be exposed."

Alan chirps in "At Danny's behest we've already had the video removed from the internet."

Ashton "Wow, feel that. My dick just twitched. No pun intended Alan. Keep this up Danny and I may have to rush home early. Now, I want to be kept informed of everything relating to this. Understood?"

Danny "Sure Ashton."

Ashton "OK, don't forget we have that thing tonight at The Katling. I want what's left of your team there reassuring all our investors and creditors that everything is not just hunky dory, but fucking great. See you tonight," he looks down to see who is next on his list. Danny gets up and nods to Alan and Reg. He leaves the room wondering how he will convince Iris and Susan to leave their homes let alone attend an Investor party with over two hundred people. Maybe the increased security could convince them or just the fact that if they don't show, Ashton will likely fire them in an instant. "Yep" that's the way to go, "Nothing like the fear of losing a six figure salary to instil obedience."

Susan, Iris and DI Blaine are in Roger's office. DI Blaine is on the phone to DI James,

"Sure no problem" he says and continues "Can you tell me what the findings are?" Blaine listens to the response then says "OK, sure, well let me know asap please" he puts the phone down and looks at Iris.

Iris impatiently "Well, what she say?"

Blaine "We've traced the transfers, but couldn't say at present who the account holders are."

Iris "Why"?

Blaine "I don't know. She just said we have to follow International Banking protocol to get the information we need."

Susan is puzzled "Following what protocol? That sounds like bullshit to me" Danny enters the office.

Iris "The police have traced the transfers, but are playing coy with the information. Do something Danny, I want that maniac locked up."

Danny looks at DI Blaine "Why are you withholding this from us?"

DI Blaine "I assume the information needs to be confirmed before we can act on it Mr Havers, in the meantime can I suggest we assign a PC to each of you till we are sure who it is we are after."

Danny looks at Iris and Susan, all of them picking up on the "Until we are sure" bit. Danny realises that unless they have definite proof that David is alive and killing, the police will always be suspicious as to their involvement. He has to find David.

Danny "That won't be necessary. The Company is arranging security for us before we leave today."Susan shakes her head in disbelief that her life has changed so much in a few days.

Susan "How can anyone have knocked out all those people at the care home? He must have used a drug or some kind of gas. Why have your Forensics not identified what it is?" Susan's frustration is hard to hide now. Fear, helplessness and anger come together to create an emotional avalanche not familiar to Susan. Her usual laid back, calm exterior is demolished, exposing a fragile and confused woman who in her heart knew what they did to David would one day come back to haunt them. She expected Karma would come knocking, but never expected it to take this form.

DI Blaine "Nothing yet."

Susan now angry "Well what the fuck do you know? Or can't you share that with us. You are treating us like suspects" as she says the words she remembers the police are still open minded about the killer.

DI Blaine looks at Susan and comments "We paid Todd's ex-wife a visit. She mentioned that you all were involved in a takeover or merger which went pear shaped, but more so for Todd. Maybe if you gave me some more details about this deal we can understand what his motivation is."

Danny, Susan and Iris look at each other. Danny takes a deep breath and clears his throat,

"I can't give you chapter and verse due to the sensitive nature of some of the companies involved, but broadly speaking we were administering a takeover and a merger which involved three companies. The deal was formally agreed subject to contracts. David was our team leader as he had always been. He had a massive investment in one of the companies involved, a fact which was disclosed. On the day the deal was to be finalised one of the companies withdrew which sent all their share prices into free fall. David lost a lot. The company he was invested in was a microchip designer which was to provide the licensing on all the military grade components. At the last minute another company entered the picture. They were able to provide the same service at a third of the cost. They got the license. I'm sure you can imagine what happened next."

DI Blaine "Strange that the lastminute.com company didn't feature earlier in the process. Who brought this company to the table?"

Danny takes another deep breath "Actually it was Dee and myself" he waits for a response from the policewoman observing her face closely.

DI Blaine "Why didn't you just tell Todd about the new company?"

Danny "Up until the very day we did not know they would go for it. If we had tried to get David to meet with them he would have said no. He was hell bent on using the company he was invested in because he knew that within ten years his investment would treble. Now he blames all of us for his greedy blinkered approach to that deal."

DI Blaine makes notes in his note book. She looks up "How much did he lose?"

Iris "Who? David?"

DI Blaine "Yes, David."

Iris looks at Susan and shifts uncomfortably in her seat "I think Susan was more familiar with the numbers."

Susan hesitates, thinks for a moment then reels off the amount "David lost seventy eight million pounds give or take a few hundred thousand."

"Sweet Jesus" The look on DI Blaine's face is a combination of bewilderment and difficulty to grasp just how much money that is.

DI Blaine "Just how much money do you people make?"

"That was everything David had accumulated over twelve years, bonuses, stock options, commission, I mean everything," Susan's voice trails off realising what she is saying.

DI Blaine raises his eyebrows "OK, now we know why. Did any of you or the others lose any money too?"

Danny takes this one "No, we didn't."

Blaine "How come, if it was such a great deal, why weren't you all piling in?"

Danny "David was long time invested and his interests were declared. Insider trading rules prohibited us from as you say, piling in" Danny hopes the Detective's lack of knowledge in this area will stop him asking more questions.

Blaine "His ex mentioned that he offered her money to see his children, any idea how a homeless and penniless man would suddenly would suddenly come into money?"

Iris "Could be anything, maybe he had a forgotten option which matured or maybe he remembered an old stock certificate, could be anything."

Susan walks over to the board table and sits. Her eyes welling up she looks at Blaine,

"He actually offered Mary money to see his children? What did she say?"

Blaine "She refused and sent him packing."

Danny looks at Iris and moves to ensure Susan does not suddenly break down with Blaine in the room "Well, if you have no further questions, we have a very important meeting to attend this evening and with all that has been going on we are pushed to get prepped Inspector."

Blaine "I understand. If I get any fresh information I'll be in touch." Blaine leaves the office closing the door on his way out.

Iris goes first "Bodyguards? Now we have to be guarded twenty four seven? Jesus Danny, this fucking mess gets worse and worse. We need to come clean to the police and Ashton and let the police plaster David's picture all over the media."

Danny is surprised, he expected something like this from the weaker Susan but not the cut throat Iris "We bribed politicians and broke god knows how many other laws to make what we did. Do you think you'd look good in prison issue gear?"

Iris "Do you really think we are going to be able to enjoy what we made for the remainder of our lives. Three of us are dead; David is out there plotting and waiting. He moves around like he is invisible, untouchable. Even the police didn't think he existed till they spoke to Mary. So no I don't want to go to prison, but I don't want to be dead either. They may not wear Prada in prison, but I'd be a much better fucking colour form what I saw of Roger."

Any other time Danny would have found what Iris said hilarious, but he sees the effect the conversation is having on Susan. She has a tear trickling down her left cheek and he needs to stop it now "OK, first of all let's agree to the bodyguards for tonight. Let's go to the do tonight and put on our best faces. If the police don't have anything concrete by midday tomorrow we go to them and Ashton with everything, but you let me present the information to limit our exposure. Agree?"

Susan and Iris look at each other and nod.

Danny "Great, now let's get together in twenty."

9 It Wasn't Personal

At 5pm Iris, Susan and Danny leave their offices accompanied by their respective bodyguards. It speaks volumes that an Investment Bank has an account with a firm who are able to supply the relevant manpower at a moment's notice. All three men are ex-military and conform to the stereotypical squared jaw broad shouldered don't fuck with me type. All three are licensed to carry firearms and all three are well trained in the use of said firearms. Most of the training gained in the service of Queen and country. Each of these guardian angels comes with a blacked out German engineered car and driver. The cars pull up outside the front of the building and one by one the packages are escorted to each vehicle. When they arrive home they are again escorted to the door and the homes searched and given the all clear before the packages can enter and relax; safe in the knowledge that there is a well armed fully trained killer at the front door waiting to stop a deranged psychopathic ex-city banker from making a bloody mess of the package. Each package is issued with a panic button, which will beckon the guardian angel immediately to dispense justice on any and all who dare to tamper with the package.

The kitchen of Iris's home is still a crime scene. The company has many apartments and town houses around the middle of London. She liked the Bayswater address because the apartment is on the top floor making it safer. With the angel at the door and the driver outside she feels safer now than at any time in the past few days. She draws a hot bath and laces it with fine oils and soaps. She sinks into the bath and reaches for a glass of white wine.

Iris's angel is a thirty six year old, six foot two well muscled ex-marine. It was hard being a mixed race soldier when he first enlisted, but these days more and more youngsters were taking the opportunity as a way off the benefits and the streets. He had done his term and knew what he wanted to do when he left. The money was great and ninety five percent of the time there was no trouble. They were there more for prevention than cure. Nevertheless he always wore an expensive and discrete vest under his expensive and less discrete suit. He positioned himself outside the apartment door in order to observe the lift and stairs at the same time.

The driver is parked on the street with eyes on the building front door. The rear door to the building was secured from the inside and would be difficult to open from the outside. Difficult, but not impossible. He positions a motion detector beam about knee high to at least get a heads up if anyone tries to enter via a door which should not normally be used. His phone buzzes and he answers "How many?" he asks the driver.

Iris' angel "OK, in the lift now" he ends the call. Someone enters the lift and the lift squeaks its way upward. It gets to the third floor, Iris' floor. The doors open and an old man in an oversized grey coat steps out. He is laden with two of those ten pence Sainsbury shopping bags and a baguette under his right arm. As he steps out and moves towards the angel heading to one of the other apartments. He favours his right leg limping as he moves. He drops the bread as his right leg gives slightly. The angel moves toward him to help. The old man rests the bags on the floor and accepts the angel's help.

"Thank you son, these old knees are not what they used to be" the old man complains.

He is about seventy with a bushy grey beard. Fully clothed for a harsh winter he tries to straighten up. He sighs heavily and curses as he takes in his surroundings.

"Wrong fucking floor again. I'm on the second."

The angel helps him reload and escorts him to the lift. The old man enters the lift and presses the button for the second floor. The door closes and the angel returns to his duty.

He calls the driver "Hi, keep an eye out; let me know when an old man in a grey coat leaves. Yeah, same guy. Thanks."

Susan's and Danny's cars arrive at Danny's Battersea tower block apartment at the same time. The drivers ensured that. Most people expect Danny to be the more central type, but he had bought off-plan when development in the area was in its infancy. His bet paid off. There was now a stretch of high end stupidly expensive apartment blocks along the river. Many of the apartments were purchased by overseas investors and just kept empty. Danny's was a penthouse with two bedrooms, two reception rooms a study and a kitchen diner. Initially he had hired a local interior designer simply because he wanted fuck her, and when he did, he sacked her and hired the services of a much less attractive, but far more talented designer.

As Susan, Danny and the angels exit the cars and approach the block, the Concierge opens the door for them.

"Good evening Mr Havers, Miss Chang."

Danny "Evening Ronin, we have a couple of gentlemen who will be keeping an eye out for us tonight and the two cars and drivers will be here also. Can you let them have any assistance they need?"

Ronin came to the UK three years earlier from Rome. Ronin wasn't his real name, but he thought it gave him an air of mystery. Just what a Concierge needs.

Ronin a little puzzled "Sure thing Mr Havers" he closes the door and Danny, Susan and one angel go to the lifts. The other angel speaks to Ronin

"Anyone entering the building you don't know you call this number" he hands him a card "Show me the rear of the building and I need to know what security system you have."

"OK sir" feeling more than just a little uneasy.

As they return from the exploratory mission the phone on Ronin's desk rings. He answers it.

"Oh, Hi Mike, yeah I got you in the book for tomorrow morning at 7 am. Cool, see you then" he hangs up.

Angel "Who was that?"

"Maintenance guy."

"Call me when he arrives."

"OK sir" he felt like saluting.

The angel makes a call to the drivers and then heads to the lifts to join his colleague on the penthouse floor.

Ronin sits at his station and whispers to himself "What the fuck."

The pressure was definitely getting to Susan, and Danny wanted to diffuse her before they arrived at The Katling. If it was Iris he knew exactly what would do it for her, but Susan was a very different person. She needed reassurances and to be transported away from it all mentally. Susan showered first and was sat on the bed when Danny entered still drying himself.

"How are you holding up? Need a neck massage?"

"Really Danny? Now?"

Danny innocently "What?"

"By massage you mean sex, or a blow job or whatever."

Danny even more innocently "Seriously babe, I can see how upset you are, the last thing on my mind is sex. I just want you to be a little more relaxed before we go out tonight. This is a very important night for us. We are three men down and Ashton is really relying on us to impress the shit out of the investors tonight."

Susan apologetically "I'm sorry Danny, it's just so much happening so quickly."

"I know, now lie down and I'll get some oil" Danny goes to the bathroom to get some oil and a couple of condoms.

The Katling, a Boutique Hotel owned by the bank. Opulent and very private, all meetings, celebrations and functions were under the highest of security. All staff and visitors were fully vetted and scrutinised by the same security company providing tonight's angels. Iris wanted Danny and Susan to arrive first. She felt odd not being accompanied by Roger.

Danny is fully tuxed up and Susan is in a light blue low cut cocktail dress which emphasises her figure and tanned skin. For a woman on the verge of a breakdown she looked amazing. Hair down and smiling as she and Danny greet the assembled assortment of Company CEOs, CFOs, Chairmen, Bankers, Brokers and generally anyone who if you scratched their back would return the favour to ensure the gravy train for the elite keeps on chugging. Not so much the little engine that could more like a high speed unstoppable bullet train that will.

About ten minutes after Danny and Susan arrive, so does Iris. Knowing that she has to dress to impress without looking slutty she chooses an ankle length number with a low back and high front. The slit up to her thigh provided the provocative element to the outfit. Hair up because she knew Susan's would be down, Iris oozed class and as she schmoozed she gained a fan base.

Ashton's voice booms into a huddled conversation between Iris, Susan, Danny and two of the principle investors "Ah, there's my A Team!" Ashton approaches the group with a stunning young woman attached to his left arm. Danny's eyes widen, he had never met Ashton's wife before; He had heard much about her but this was definitely an eye opener. She was about five feet seven, no older than twenty eight, redhead with almost ghostly white skin. Dressed in a similar dress to Iris, but filling it so much better. Iris notices Danny's eyes glazing over "Easy dickhead, that's the boss's wife" she whispers to him.

Danny whispering back "I'm not a fucking idiot, besides she's nothing compared to you" Danny is fixated by this woman. As he gapes at her he becomes aware that he has not heard a word after Ashton's initial hail.

He averts his eyes back to Ashton and hears "I'm informed all is on track for two days time, right Danny?"

Danny "Absolutely Ash."

A voice from outside the group says "What about the death of three of the team? What's that all about? Should we be worried Ashton?"

Ashton smiles and turns to Tom Hillier CEO of Mantech. News of the takeover had seen the company's valuation almost triple what the real market cap should be.

Ashton "Tom, as you all know I've kept everyone in the loop on this to ensure this deal is not jeopardised. All the numbers have been crunched and the paperwork prepped and ready to sign. Funds are allocated and from what I saw this morning Mantech share price is now triple what it was five weeks ago, making you a very rich man."

Tom "Better keep these three safe till then Ashton, we've spent a lot of money getting here. Money paid to your company."

Ashton gently loosens his wife's arm and walks over to Tom; he beckons a waiter over holding a tray of filled champagne glasses. Ashton takes two from the tray, hands one to Tom and turns to the group.

"To MantechAKM, a new and exciting company set to drive the development and deployment of military and domestic robotic technology now and in the future, Cheers." Everyone raises their glasses and drink.

The night progresses well. The team circulates saying the right things and instilling confidence that the deal is all done subject to signatures and the moving of a lot of money. The angels keep an eye on their charges and a second set of angels are dispatched to keep an eye on the homes.

Somehow Danny finds himself standing alone with Ashton's wife "Apparently you are responsible for my husband's lack of desire in the bedroom department."

Ashton's wife Ellie came from Ireland to London when she was seventeen. She met and married Ashton when she was twenty two. She married for the money and Ashton knew it.

Danny "I don't see how anyone can possibly lack desire especially if you're in the bedroom."

"You flirting with me?"

"No, just saying it as I see it" as he finishes the words Danny realises he has a strong desire to touch this woman. Not like on the face or hold her hand, but to touch her in more intimate places. He looks at her breast, her plunging neckline exposing so much of her boobs as to leave very little to the imagination. Her milky white skin, so soft looking. Just one touch, just a gentle stroke, perhaps a fondle. Something is wrong, Danny feels it. He can't stop looking at her boobs "Danny, my eyes are up here" Ellie is starting to get a little uneasy. Danny suddenly feels his right arm involuntarily start to rise and knows where it is heading. He can hear Aston's voice in the background and will probably be about to feel his fist on the back of his head. As his arm rises heading towards Ellie's left tit Iris jumps in.

"Ah, Danny there you are. Tom needs some more information on the stock split" she grabs Danny's arm and turns him away from Ellie "Sorry Ellie, business is business."

Ellie "No problem" still unsure as to whether that was an awkward moment or not.

Iris admonishes Danny "What the fuck is wrong with you arsehole?"

Danny fazed "I'm, I'm not sure. Suddenly I just had all these thoughts and I tried to stop, but, but just couldn't."

Iris now even madder at Danny "Listen you fucking idiot, just grab Susan and get the fuck out of here. I'll make excuses and get home too. Stay the hell away from anything in a skirt. Now go."

Danny, still a bit bewildered rushes off in the direction of Susan.

He interrupts her "I think we should be making tracks my dear. Lots to do tomorrow. Early start and all that" Susan looks at Danny and assumes he's had a couple too many.

Susan "Danny's right, we have got a pretty heavy workload" she shakes hands and air kisses as appropriate whilst Danny heads to the exit. He collects their coats. Susan catches up with him. He helps her into her coat and they walk to the lobby. Their angels expertly appear and surround them in a protective shield as they exit the lobby to their car. One angel rides with them in the front passenger seat and the other in the second car with the other driver.

Minutes later Iris, angel in tow, exits The Katling and departs. She arrives at the temporary apartment and heads straight to bed. Iris slept well, better than she had done in days. For that time she forgot about the gruesome events of the last week. She even had a dream about her bodyguard. Her phone's alarm with its gentle rousing tones wakes her out of the dream. She curses the alarm for spoiling the ending for her. She throws back the quilt and steps into her slippers. The apartment is warm. She heads to the en-suite.

Danny's apartment. His alarm goes off; the ring tone is "Who let the dogs out......"

Susan "turn that fucking thing off or I'll put a bullet in the fucking dog" she covers her head with the pillow. Danny reaches for the phone and kills the alarm. He'd been awake for about an hour thinking over what happened the night before. Couldn't have been the drink, he only had two glasses of champagne and a couple of Vodkas. Just imagine the shit storm he'd be in right now if Iris hadn't stopped him. Susan surfaces and sees him staring at the ceiling.

"What's wrong? I mean other than the obvious."

Danny puts his arm around her and draws her face to his chest "Let's just take the day off and fuck all day."

"Or we can get up, get to the office and get the police to give us what information they have on the transfers."

Danny is disappointed "I like my idea more, but yeah, what the hell" he eases himself away from Susan and heads off to the bathroom.

Susan and Danny accompanied by Derek and Jim, these angels have names, exit the lift and hear the night concierge on the phone.

"I can barely hear you. Press the intercom on the panel and I'll let you in" there is a buzzing sound, the night concierge presses a button and puts the phone down.

Danny "Morning Gary, uneventful night I hope."

Gary "Certainly was, just the maintenance guy arriving a little early."

Derek "Can you just check his ID; make sure he is the person you are expecting?"

Gary "Sure, no problem" no intention of checking. His shift finishes in about five minutes and it sounds just like the maintenance guy.

Danny, Susan and the angels depart the apartment block and head to their office. Gary gets up from his desk to go pretend to check on the maintenance guy when Ronin walks in two minutes early. Gary is pleased and gets up, puts his jacket on and heads to the door.

Ronin "I'll see you tonight. Don't be late. I've got a date" Gary rushes out the door to make his bus.

Iris exits her apartment hoping to see her guardian angel, but disappointed to find he was replaced during the night by a much older but equally confidence inspiring angel.

"Good morning Mam, my name is Joel, I'll be looking out for you today" Joel has a surprisingly soft voice. Iris sizes him up quickly. White male about forty five, six two, slim but probably in great shape. Shaved head, impassionate face, probably doesn't smile much "To the office?"

Iris "Yes" she is ushered to the lift. The lift door opens and they proceed to exit the building.

As the lift arrives on the ground floor the doors open and there is the old man from the previous day waiting. He is hunched over holding a Sainsbury carrier bag. Iris and Joel exit the lift and the old man enters.

Iris "Who's that?" she is on high alert.

Joel "He lives on the second floor. We've checked him out. He's lived here for the past eight years."

Iris "Oh."

They get in the car and head to the office.

8:00 am in front of the offices of AKM. DI Blaine and James are parked across the road watching as the various staff members arrive. They watch as Susan and Danny arrive along with their entourage. Iris follows soon after. James is in the driver's seat. She looks at the print out and shakes her head.

James "Still hard to believe, why he would do all this and still stick around. Doesn't make sense."

Blaine "I guess he enjoys it and wants to watch them up close and personal. Come on, let's talk to them."

They get out of the car leaving a laminate with the words "Police Vehicle" on the dash. They head to the AKM office building.

In the boardroom Ashton is seated with his trusted advisors on either side. Iris, Susan and Danny are at the table to his right and Tom Hillier at the table to his left. Tom also has a team of trusted advisors, four in total present.

Ashton "Thank you all for coming here this morning. I know I struggled a little after last night, but I had a great time and I hope you all did too" some nod their heads in acknowledgement and some just smile. Ashton continues "We've got a couple of minor points to put to bed and we can finalise the contracts for tomorrow's signing" he smiles and looks to Danny to take over.

As Danny is about to speak Ashton's secretary enters the boardroom "Sorry Sir, but they were insistent" DI Blaine and James follow her into the boardroom.

Ashton annoyed "What the fuck is this, we're in the middle of a very important meeting."

Blaine "We are sorry for the intrusion, but I think you will all find this very revealing Mr Carter."

Ashton "If this is about David Todd then we don't need to have Tom and his team here. Just wait outside and when we are done I will call you in."

James "Actually it may be relevant to the Mantech representatives also."

Iris "Our problems with David have nothing to do with this deal" as she finishes the sentence she is curious to know what they have and where this is going.

Ashton "You can't make assumptions which are likely to impact on a multi billion pound deal officers er.." Ashton tries to recall the name.

Blaine helps Ashton out "James and Blaine. We have proof that shows one man is responsible for the murders of your staff members and others."

Danny sits up "David Todd, right? Finally you believe us now."

James "No Mr Havers, in fact we were unable to link Mr Todd to any of the incidents. No witnesses, nothing on CCTV and no prints or DNA. A further fact is that much of what we have actually points the finger in your direction."

The entire room goes silent. Danny looks up at the detectives and begins to laugh with disbelief. Iris and Susan look at Danny then each other. Ashton stands up and walks to the police officers.

Ashton, angry now "What the fuck is this? Are you trying to sabotage this deal? Who are you working for?"

DI Blaine "Mr Carter, look at the money trail. We have transfers from Mr Patel, Mr Caldwell and Mr Howard accounts to overseas accounts in Dubai and Singapore. The Dubai accounts are for companies set up five years ago and with the sole director listed as Mr Havers. We have not been able to trace all the information from the Singapore transfers and are probably not likely to based on the complexity of the set up and the lack of transparency with the Singapore banking regulations."

Danny springs to his feet "This is a fucking set up. Why would I leave a trail to myself on one hand and on the other use an alternative which is untraceable?"

James "We wondered that too, so we did a bit of checking into the shell companies and found something very interesting. We cross referenced all of the deceased names, yours, Miss Chang and Mrs Caldwell also against offshore companies and we got a hit on all of you. All companies started about five years ago within approximately six months of each other and all used to trade in a specific UK based company via a broker in Frankfurt."

Danny, Iris and Susan all realise what the officers are leading up to.

James continues as she walks up to Danny "They were all shorting shares in Genova, the very same company this investment bank was administering a takeover for and subsequently lost more than seventy percent of its value in less than three days."

Ashton takes the papers from Blaine and reads them carefully.

Danny "That's bullshit. This is a setup. I don't know how, but David is setting us up. Ashton I swear .." Ashton cuts Danny's plea short.

"You're a fucking traitor Danny. It's all here. The companies, the trades, everything. You set David up. You fucking set me up. You and everyone else working for him."

Ashton turns to Blaine "Well, what are you waiting for? Arrest them."

Blaine "We can't, we are waiting for our people to define exactly what to charge them for. We can't link him to the murders directly yet and our Fraud team are still investigating exactly what laws have been broken. We can't arrest anyone yet."

Tom Hillier has been sitting still, stunned by the events unfolding in the boardroom.

"What about the deal? What the hell does this mean for my company?"

James clears her throat as if she is about to deliver something she'd rather not "Well we found some trades which kind of mirror what happened in the past."

Tom confused "Please just spit it out."

James "We found several shorts against Mantech. These were placed a few days ago, again using the same companies and broker as before," Ashton's mobile rings, so does Tom's.

Ashton recognises the number and answers it immediately "Yes?" there is brief moment as Tom answers his mobile also and slowly rises to his feet. He lowers his phone to the table ending the call at the same time.

Tom "That was my office; news is out that the merger has collapsed and police are investigating a potential impropriety. Our stock is down thirty percent and falling" he sinks back into his seat.

Ashton "Yeah, I know." He turns to his secretary "I want these three out of this building in the next ten minutes. Make sure all their accesses are revoked and set up a meeting with the Regulators."

Iris "Danny, what the fuck is this. Do something."

Danny's mind is racing. He can't understand how everything just fell apart so quickly. Four security guards appear at the boardroom door. Two for Danny and one each for Iris and

Susan. Susan hasn't said anything since the evidence of their betrayal was produced. She just keeps thinking "Karma, karma" as if she knew that one day this would happen.

Ashton "Get these scumbags out of here. No contact with anyone. Just get them out now."

Everyone watches as the three are escorted out of the room directly to the corridor.

Tom "This has happened before? On your watch?" he is beyond angry.

Ashton reasserts his control "Not now Tom. Sit the fuck down and let's work out a settlement" he addresses the police officers "If you have nothing else can you please excuse us? We have a few things to discuss." The officers leave.

David Todd is sitting in the kitchen of his flat with a laptop on the kitchen table. He smiles as he observes the Mantech share price drop a further ten percent to below forty percent of its previous day's closing price "Just business."

10 Acedia

Danny, Susan and Iris are sitting in a coffee shop two blocks from the office they have just been ejected from. Still stunned by the morning's events they stare at the hot drinks which have just been delivered to the table. Danny is desperately trying to piece it all together. He knows the harsh truth is that he and the others have been rumbled. David dropped huge lumps of bread crumbs for the police to follow and assemble a meatloaf at the end of the trail. Four hours ago they were being escorted by bodyguards. Twenty minutes ago the bodyguards were replaced by building security.

Iris lets out a sigh "What now? No job, under investigation for fraud and murder, my husband is dead; what now Danny?"

Danny has a light bulb moment "We go on the attack. We know who is behind the killings, but we were constrained by adverse publicity from going to the press."

Susan can see his point "He's right. We couldn't go to the press before, but there is nothing to stop us now. What about the police? The press will contact them to confirm David is a person of interest."

Danny "We all have alibis for all the incidents. The police know that or else we'd be answering questions right now. Your husband has been killed. Three prominent figures in a prominent London Investment Bank have been brutally murdered. The press will lap this up. We need to get David's picture out there. That fucker is nearby and with all the eyes of London looking out, there is a better than good chance he will be spotted."

Iris "True, worst case scenario he is spooked and disappears" she pauses for a moment and continues "We need to do this now."

Susan "I need to get back to the apartment. We're unemployed now and if I know Ashton there is no way in hell any of us will ever work in The City again. I just want to cash in some investments and make sure David can't do what he did to the others."

Danny "Susan is right. We need to consolidate. David has been one step ahead of us and he won't stop till we are dead or in the gutter with him. We need to stay together though. We can go to my place first then to yours Iris. Then we book a couple of hotel rooms and make contact with the press. They leave their beverages unfinished and exit the coffee shop.

David is lying on the bed in his City pad. He bought a pay as you go phone with a camera few days ago and has been torn between videoing Shithead or not. What if he took the video and looked at it and saw nothing in the box. That would mean he is completely off his trolley and a psychopath to boot. So far Shithead had done all the heavy lifting while he just savoured the sweet taste of revenge. He was close to concluding his business with his ex-colleagues and reclaiming his life. Maybe not as it was before, but a darn sight better than it had been in the last four years.

David sits up and pulls the box from under the bed. Every time he does this he expects the thing to not be there, but there it is.

Wriggling and impatient he hears its voice in his head.

"Now, we have some fun" David knows what it wants to do and gets up off the bed. He heads to the small wardrobe in the corner of the room, opens it and takes his jacket and coat out. He dresses and picks up the box from the bed.

"I know, I know, you don't have to keep repeating yourself." He puts the box back under the bed, turns the light out and leaves the flat.

Iris had packed light for her temporary accommodation in the company apartment. Ashton sent one of the AKM security guards to ensure she vacated with maximum haste. Danny had a friend at The Landmark who reserved a couple of Suites for them. The suites were next to each other but not adjoining. Susan and Danny are unpacking in the bedroom.

The Landmark is one of those old hotels where tradition, mahogany and patterned carpets are combined with five star service and customer care. Not exactly lying low, but no one other than Danny's contact at the hotel knows they are there.

Susan sits on the bed and glances at her watch. 3:30 pm, she usually has a call from her mum or dad by now. As she reaches for her phone it rings.

It's her father "Hi Sue, I tried calling you at work, but they say you not working there anymore. You leave job?"

Unable to deal with any more awkwardness today Susan lies "No dad, I'm just working from home today. Is everything OK?" she kind of listens as her father reels of a list of complaints "OK Dad I'll pop over in an hour to have a look. Is mum there?"

"No she coming later. I see you later then" he hangs up and Danny sits on the bed next to her.

"I'll come with you."

"No need, he got some papers relating to the restaurant in the post. Wants me to have a look" Susan is actually looking forward to getting away from Danny, Iris and the issues "I'll take a cab there and back, no more than a couple of hours. When are we meeting with the newspaper?"

"I spoke with the Telegraph and they will have someone over at 6pm today. You sure you'll be back in time?"

"If I know my father it's probably just something to do with the rates."

Susan is about to order an Uber, but she feels the need to walk and clear her head. She puts on her coat and leaves the apartment. She walks to the bus stop and waits for the No 38. By bus it would take her about thirty minutes. The bus arrives as predicted by the TFL app. It's a new double decker hybrid. The doors open and she boards the bus, waves her contactless bank card over the payment machine, and moves into the bus to find a seat. The lower section is pretty full. Lots of people heading into London for a bit of Christmas shopping. The only available seat is a Priority Seat for people with pushchairs, the elderly and the disabled. She hates sitting on these because people always look even though she would give up the seat instantly for a qualifying person. She hates standing up in the bus too. Far too many times she has been inappropriately touched. Knowing the bus will get fuller as it moves closer to Central London she opts to take the seat for now.

Susan settles into the seat next to a short black woman who looks in her early seventies. The old lady is bundled up in her coat with a woollen hat on her head. She is holding a walking stick in her right hand and in front of her is a shopping trolley that a lot of old people use to wheel their shopping about. There is no eye contact or acknowledgement of each other's presence. The old lady stares out the window and Susan looks ahead.

Two stops later the bus is now fairly full and luckily those standing are young and healthy. Third stop and Susan hears "Need a hand mate?" a sure sign she will now have to stand. The crowd of young and healthy part to allow a man, who looks about in his early forties, through. He is limping with a walking stick. He is big. Big as in fat "Big." Susan guesses he must be about twenty four stones and standing only about five feet six it shows on him. She knows it's time to relinquish the seat to the qualifier heading over. She attempts to stand, but she can't. Her mind and spirit are willing but her body just won't obey. She pushes hard up again and again as the man shuffles through heading directly to her. He has already locked on to his target and is moving with a certainty that the seat will be his. Susan tries again, but no joy.

"Shit! Shit!" she thinks "I've got to move."

As she fails to even budge slightly she starts to panic a little. People are starting to look at her. She tries to reach out to grab the pole in front of her, but her arms won't move either. The man is five feet from her and she hasn't stood up yet. The young and healthy start to see a situation brewing. The old lady next to Susan nudges her with her left elbow and gestures to the shuffling man with her head basically saying "Oi, qualifying person for the Priority Seat. Get the fuck up." Susan is visibly shaking in her efforts to vacate the damn seat. Then it happens, the man is directly in front of her with an expectant look on his face. Susan tries again and again, but nothing. She looks up at the man. Up close she realises she was mistaken. This is in fact a young man about mid twenties but with obvious physical and from the features of his face possibly mental issues.

He looks at her and utters a simple "Please Miss." Susan is sweating now.

She looks at him and says "I'm so very, very sorry, but I can't move."

The young and healthy along with the rest of the lower deck are flabbergasted.

The old lady is first to go in a thick West Indian accent "Why you don't let the boy sit. You can see he is not well."

Susan still feverishly still trying to stand "I'm sorry I just can't" not realising her words are interpreted quite differently by her observers "I'm trying, but I can't."

A Polish man sitting directly behind Susan speaks up "Lady, you can have my seat just let the boy sit."

Susan shouts at the Polish man "I'm trying to stand' but I can't you stupid man" now all of the lower deck are alert to a situation.

The driver looks at his on board camera screen and switches on the PA microphone "Everything OK back there?"

Old West Indian lady "No it's not. There is a woman here who won't give up the Priority seat for this poor boy driver. You have to get her off this bus now."

Susan quickly responds "I want to get up but" then suddenly she thinks to herself "this boy is so fucking fat he could do with some exercise; even it's just standing" there is a huge gasp from the passengers as Susan realises she didn't just think it, she said it out loud.

The boy starts to well up and that sends more passengers into mob mode.

Susan hears "Get the fuck up bitch or we'll throw you off" one of the young and healthy is pointing his phone at her.

"This is so going on YouTube."

Old West Indian lady "You don't get your rass up, I'm gonna slap your blasted face!"

The driver exits his cockpit and approaches the problem "Let me through please" he gets there and looks at Susan. The driver is a portly mixed race man in his mid thirties with a South London accent "Lady, please get up unless you satisfy the condition to sit here."

Susan, now no longer in control of her legs and mouth "Maybe if he takes a good look at you, and sees what he could look like in ten years, he might appreciate a little standing time."

Driver "You can insult me all you want, but please get up or get off the bus. We're not moving till you do one or the other" there is a collective "Oh man!" followed by shouting from passengers. The top deck is now peering down the stairs to find out what the problem is.

Driver "OK Lady I'm going to call the police. Maybe you'll see it differently when they arrive" as the driver is about to turn to head back to the cockpit Susan suddenly stands bolt upright.

Her legs are back "Let me off the bus please" she walks the three feet to the door being nudged and bumped by passengers as she does. The Driver reaches for a small handle above the door, turns it and the doors open. She steps off the bus and hears the other passengers cheering and applauding.

Susan gets her phone out and hails an Uber. 4:25 pm outside the Jade Garden Restaurant. Susan's cab pulls up and she gets out. Still shaken from the bus incident she really just wants to get back to the apartment and tell Danny what happened. She has never experienced anything like that before, but she promised her father.

She looks at the darkened restaurant front as she exits the cab. Why her father had chosen this quiet location to open a restaurant was beyond her.

"People will come for excellent food" he kept saying.

It is a big restaurant occupying two fronts. Decorated in green and red it shouts "Chinese restaurant!" Her father has forgotten to put on the night lights by the look of it. The restaurant doesn't open till 6:30pm but the sign and some of the interior lights are usually on. She gets her keys out and opens the door to the ornate porch then the main restaurant door.

"Dad? I'm here" she expects her dad to pop his head round the corner from the kitchen as he always does, but not today. With all that has been going on and seeing Michael's mother become a victim she is suddenly worried.

"Dad? Are you in the kitchen? Mum?" she cautiously approaches the door to the kitchen. There is a dim light on in the kitchen. She curses herself for not putting the restaurant light on.

As she creeps up to the door she hears a familiar voice "Hello Susan" she stops.

The fear in her goes from level four to ten instantly. It's David.

He's here "Looking for someone Susan? Someone you care about perhaps?"

Susan can't see David. She peers into the dark room at the direction the voice came from.

"David? That you?" she asks almost by instinct, her heart beating so loudly she thinks he might hear it.

David calmly "Yes Susan. It's me. Good to see you again. Come sit with me." A lighter strikes up and she sees David sitting in a booth with his back to the wall. She slowly walks over to the booth wanting desperately to ask where her father and mother are. As she reaches the booth David lights a candle and extinguishes the lighter flame "Sit down, we have a lot to catch up on" she shuffles into the opposite seat.

"Where are my parents?"

David waits a moment and leans forward to get a good look at her "Safe" he lets that soak in wondering if she believes him "What happens next is entirely up to you."

"David, I know you know what we did and for that I am truly sorry. You trusted us and we took advantage of that trust."

David still calm "I'm so glad you see it that way, but what I want is to examine what exactly your role in this was. Why is it that we are sat here in your parents restaurant, by the way I googled reviews for this place and I got to say, they weren't very encouraging, but we'll circle back to that later, as I was saying, sat here in this very dark place in our lives."

"Where are my parents David?"

"Like I said. Safe. What? You don't trust me? You think I'm some kind of back stabbing asshole? You know, the sort of people you hang around with?" David allows himself a little chuckle thinking of Dee briefly.

Susan leans in on her elbows "Please David, my parents had nothing to do with this. Just tell me where they are."

"We'll come to your parents in time. First let's take a close look at you. You are a hard working, reliable mathematician. You're not a physically lazy person, you deal with any work you are asked to do efficiently, but you have a flaw. Do you know what that is?" Susan opens her mouth about to attempt to answer David's question.

"Shut up Susan. Rhetorical question. I'm going to give you the answer" David pauses for a little dramatic effect; he has rehearsed this speech and wants to get it right "You don't like confrontation. You spend too much of your time avoiding. You will allow yourself to be walked over rather than confront another person. Now let's apply that to what you did to me."

Susan stuttering "I, I don't see..." she fumbles under the table trying to open the clasp of her handbag. Her handbag which she remembers is armed with pepper spray and an illegal taser she had bought below the counter in the corner shop two doors down last week.

"No you don't, because you can't. It's not your fault, probably genetic. Now that brings us to your parents."

She gets the clasp open and feels for any of the two weapons "Please leave them out of this."

"I can't. We are sitting in the very reason you turned on me. This shithole has been losing money since it opened ten years ago. You've been injecting capital every year to save your parents from having to face the shame of failure. Instead of just telling them that he is a shit cook and they both have zero business sense, you chose to let them continue to lose money and when it was so bad that closure was inevitable, Danny came up with the bright idea of stabbing me in the back to make everyone filthy rich. That meant you could continue to prop up the restaurant till you managed to gumption up and tell mummy and daddy what the reality is. How am I doing?"

Tears drip down Susan's cheeks, partly because she knows what David said is dead on and partly because she can't find the spray or taser in her bag.

"I'll do anything. Please, I have money; you can have whatever I have."

David shakes his head "Whatever you have came from me you little bitch. That money came from my misery. Let's talk about what that money cost me and stop searching the bag; they're not in there."

Susan sits back placing the bag on the table. All along he knew she was searching her bag. How'd he know what was in there? She needed to appeal to the old David. The David who was her friend, the David she once kissed at a Christmas party and regretted it immediately after.

She needs to regain some of his trust "We've all been fired. The police and Ashton know what happened four years ago" she stops short at telling him about the meeting with the newspaper then realises this may be her last few moments alive "Danny and Iris are meeting with a journalist later to get them to run a story on you as the killer."

"Really? The hunted want to do some hunting?"

"I can give you money and help you get over to France. From there you can get" David cuts in,

"I don't need your money. What I want is revenge" David, his voice raised "What I want is what I had. Do you hear what I'm saying Susan?" She is crying; he's just not listening.

"Now as lovely as this restaurant is I think we should move to the kitchen. You know; surprise the chef" David smiles. He hadn't expected to have any fun on this one, but the more he spoke to Susan the more he realised she was no different to the others. She used the same tactics they did to get out of the situation. He wondered what he would do if the roles were reversed. As David stands up Susan wants to strike out at him; punch, slap anything that could stop him moving to the kitchen and her seeing what she fears the most. As hard as she tries she just can't, she remembers the bus incident and wonders if David was somewhere on the bus then too. Unable to do anything else she obeys David's "request" to move to the kitchen. Susan exits the booth and slowly heads toward the kitchen doors. She opens the doors and enters the kitchen. The kitchen is large with a wok station accommodating up to five cooks. There are separate areas for prepping and cleaning. It is a very clean and well organised kitchen. The addition four years ago of a large walk in bespoke oven to make roast duck was one of the more sensible ideas. This oven was able to roast up to forty duck at a time which meant that the restaurant could sell to other proprietors in the area.

As Susan enters the kitchen she hears her father's voice ask "Who there?"

Susan "Dad where are you? It's me" David switches the lights on. Susan gasps. She sees her father standing by the wok station.

Then she hears another voice "Baby, is that you?" It's her mother.

Susan lets out a huge sob "Mummy, no please David."

David watches her reaction carefully. Some part of him is fascinated to know which parent's potential peril would evoke the strongest emotional response in Susan. Susan's mother is standing just past an island used for prepping. She is standing by an electric meat grinder. There are tears streaming down her cheeks.

Susan knows she has to get it together if her family are to get out of this kitchen alive. She takes a couple of deep breaths and appeals again to David "Please, this is between us, Please just leave them out of it" images of Michael's mother come to her vividly.

David walks up to the island which positions him so he can observe Susan, her mum and dad easily "It does involve them."

"No, they had nothing to do with it."

"Not directly, but let me explain. To establish their indirect involvement we have to examine your motivation to do what you did."

Mr Chang "Susan, what going on here. Who this man. He say he an Accountant then he make us do things. This man cursed. This Demon work."

Mrs Chang "Baby, we can't move. I think he drugged us."

David "I wish I had gagged you both too. Now shut the fuck up so I can explain to your baby here why we are all in this kitchen" David pauses then continues "Now, where was I? Ah, motivation, specifically yours Susan. I came into the restaurant a few days ago and pretended to be an Accountant. To cut a long story short I offered my services to your dad for free for a year. So I had a chance to go over the business accounts. This place is a money pit. Poorly located, to big, too many staff, shit food, I could go on, but I'm sure you already know this crap. This place has never made a profit, but has been in business over ten years. How"? David waits for Susan to answer.

"I've been subsidising the restaurant. I'd inject capital to keep it going whenever it needed it."

"That right, now with good ole dad's really quite shitty cooking and his reluctance to hire decent chefs you must have known that this place will always be a money pit. I know one of the female Changs does. Am I right Mrs Chang"?

Mrs Chang weeps. She dips and shakes her head slowly from side to side.

David continues "Mummy knew a long time ago, Daddy's unusually poor business acumen for a Chinese businessman would put them on the street, so she devised a little plan to divert some of the daily cash into her handbag. That's right Mummy has been dipping into the till for years."

Susan and Mr Chang look at Mrs Chang in disbelief.

Susan "Is this true Mum"? Mrs Chang just nods her head.

Mrs Chang "I had to Susan, he was just not listening. This place was taking everything from us, from you."

Mr Chang shocked "You steal from you own family"?

David "To recap; we've got Daddy driving away customers with his piss poor cooking" David breaks off to recall something "What was that dish I had a couple of days ago? I ordered sweet and sour pork and got what tasted like sweet and stinky foot" he resumes his train of thought "As I was saying, poor cooking, bad business sense, Mummy's sticky fingers in the till and you not willing to point out the obvious to the old man."

Mr Chang angry "Fuck you Demon. I chop your fucking balls off."

David in a mocking tone "Mr Chang, not in front of Mummy and baby" David walks over to him and turns on the gas burner under one of the woks in front of Mr Chang.

Mr Chang feels a chill go through him as the burner roars into flame. The flames start to heat the wok filled to half way with oil.

Susan shouts "No, leave him alone!"

David turns to her "I'm not going to lay a finger on him. I'm guessing about five years ago you realised you couldn't keep propping up the restaurant and progress your own life, so when Danny showed you a way out you took it. Correct?"

Susan ready to bare it all "Yes. I just couldn't see my parents fail. He's just too old to start again and he needed the respect from his community. I needed a lot of money quickly."

David "And there you go. Motivation and indirect involvement. You see, we are all linked and there will be a sharing of responsibility here tonight."

David walks over to Mrs Chang. He reaches round her and switches on the grinder which whirls into life.

Susan tears still flowing, nose running "No! Please David!"

David walks back to his observation point.

"From the outside this looks like an idyllic family, but it's fucked up. So let's try a little group therapy. I'm going to help you to overcome your mental lethargy. Susan I want you to choose which parent should be punished for their involvement in my predicament."

"Please, let them go. I'll do anything you want, please David" David had read somewhere once that the more a hostage used the name of its captor the more the captor was likely to empathise with the hostages requests.

He wondered if that was what Susan has been trying
"Please David. I'm here; do what you want."

"I want you to say Mummy or Daddy baby."

Mr Chang shouts "She choose me asshole! Me!"

"She has to say it."

"Susan, say me. It OK baby. This asshole kill me I come back and cut his balls off."

David "Mr Chang you've got to stop talking about castration. It's been a long week and we're starting to run out of ideas. Now Susan! Choose now!"

Susan wants to fall to her knees, she wants to run to her Dad, she wants a hug from her Mum, but none of these things are happening.

"No, I can't, I can't."

"I'm going to count to three then if you haven't chosen I'll punish them both. One."

Mr Chang "Me you deaf asshole!"

Mrs Chang is on the verge of fainting, unable to believe the predicament they are in.

David "Two."

Susan rocks back and forth from the hip "No, no, no no, no."

David "Three!"

Susan "Dad, I'm so sorry. I'm so sorry Dad."

David "Ata girl. Dear old Dad it is then."

Susan still rocking, crying and sweating now.

David "Mr Chang, I want you to gently place your right hand into the wok in front of you."

Susan and Mrs Chang shout together "No! No!" both try to run to the old man, no joy, still can't move. With the sounds of shouting and wailing Mr Chang slowly raises his right arm and puts his hand over the now smouldering oil. He takes a deep breath and clears his mind. The voices in the background slowly fade away. He slowly lowers his hand till it is about a centimetre from the oil. The pain hits him hard. He smells his palm start to cook even before it touches the oil. Skin blistering and starting to singe. His mind is clear and in a distant place. A trick his dad had taught him to survive in the provinces. His hand enters the oil and what would ordinarily be the wonderful sound of something being placed in a hot wok was now the revolting sight of an old man shaking from the excruciating pain of being fried alive. Racked with pain his body shakes, He can see his skin crisping, the nails going an odd white. He closes his eyes and waits, hoping for a heart attack. The aroma let off is not unlike that of frying unseasoned chicken. David watches, waiting for the screaming and begging to start, but not this man. He just stands there; trembling and breathing hard while his hand is deep fried. David is both disappointed and impressed at the same time. The pain receptors and nerve endings cooked and destroyed, Mr Chang starts to only feel the pain around his wrist. After what seems like an eternity David has had enough.

David "OK. Take it out Mr Chang" Mr Chang quickly pulls his arm away from the wok.

He stares at his hand "Turn around let's all see what on tonight's specials" Mr Chang turns slowly still breathing hard and fast.

They see the hand. It looks more like a fried chicken foot "Wow, fuck me, now that's what I call a signature dish." David is please with his pun but it seems lost on the others.

David looks at Susan; she is heaving her lunch onto the kitchen floor "If you're peckish, something hot just came out of the wok" with that thought she heaves again and again.

"A lot of my money was spent in this place. I think I should at least get to try out some of the other appliances. What do you think?"

Susan expected a sense of doom to shoot through her on hearing David's words, but no, she knows they are not leaving this kitchen alive. Unless someone comes to their rescue she knows this is her last day alive.

David walks to the far side of the kitchen where the large duck roasting oven is located. He peers into the oven through the small heat proof glass window built into the door "Hmm, spacious." To the right of the door is a digital control panel.

David "All of you come here please" they comply and approach the oven.

David switches the oven on and sets the temperature to eighty Degrees Celsius. The oven's internal light comes on and illuminates the small window. David opens the door. Hot air rushes out. David is surprised and pleased by the speed the oven has taken to get hot "Get in."

Mrs Chang "No. Fuck you. Haven't you done enough?"

She looks at her husband standing to left and then at Susan on her right "We're not going in there."

David walks up to her "You really think you have a choice? I had no choice when my life was taken away by your daughter and my other friends. Get in the fucking oven bitch!"

The old man is first to move, followed by Mrs Chang. As hard as they try to resist there seems to be some sort of compulsion to obey this wicked mans orders.

As Susan moves to follow her mother David stops her "Not you."

The old man enters the oven chamber and immediately feels the heat on his face. He struggles to breathe. He moves along the chamber and Mrs Chang follows him in. David closes the door. The couple stand in the oven together and hug. Mr Chang is whispering something into his wife's ear. The oven is completely sound proofed.

David "Come here Susan, I want you to watch this." Susan is broken mentally and physically.

She moves to the small window in the door and closes her eyes.

"Open your eyes" she does. David presses the up arrow on the digital panel and the temperature read out goes from eighty to one hundred and forty. Tears flow from Susan's eyes, unable to look away as she sees the effect of the temperature increase almost immediately. Her parents hug each other harder as skin starts to bubble and spit. Their eyes closed thankfully, it not long before it's too much for them as they both collapse out of her sight. Susan retreats to a safe place. A place and time when she and her parents were happy.

David "Now it's your turn."

11 Luxuria

David returns to the lair. He's started to think of it that way since Shithead never leaves and David seems to do its bidding for all food and beverage needs. David reaches under the bed and pulls out the box. Shithead is pleased to see him. David looks at the remaining arm. Still three chubby little digits attached. Shithead expresses its need for food and tasty fluid in the usual manner and David produces a cheeseburger and Stella from a carrier bag. As he feeds the creature it talks to him.

"You want to ask me something?" David hears the voice in his head even as the creature's mouth is stuffed with food.

"It's something the old man said to me. He said I was cursed."

"Old men talk shit."

"I know, but then he started going on about Demons."

"More shit."

David coyly "Can I ask you a question?"

"No."

"Please just one question. I just need to know whether I've gone off the reservation or you are real."

Shithead is silent for about ten seconds then "One."

"What are you?"

"Does it matter?"

"That's not an answer."

"What do you think I am?"

David becoming annoyed "Just answer the fucking question and stop turning it back on me."

Shithead loudly "No! Whatever I am, you helped to create."

David shakes his head as if to clear it "OK, what if I tell you what I think you are?"

"Listening."

David sighs then continues "I think you are a psychological manifestation born of my anger and resentment against these people. I have been unable to piece the puzzle together till you started becoming a pain in my stomach and all the pieces finally fitted together when you became a pain in my arse" David is on a roll now, he'd been thinking long and hard about this "The David Todd of old would never have had the balls to do what we have been doing, so I created you to provide said balls. Right now I'm probably mushing a cheeseburger into an empty shoebox."

Shithead laughs "Heh, heh, heh" within the laugh there is perceptible message which seems to say "You poor deluded fuck."

Danny sits in his hotel suite in silence waiting for Susan and Iris to arrive before the reporter shows. He wants them to get the story right ensuring any details of their past misbehaviour are omitted. 5:15 pm and the reporter is due at six. There is knocking at the door. Its Iris, Danny opens the door first looking through the peep hole to be sure and greets her.

"Hi, come in, please" no peck on the cheek just a sombre tone "Susan popped out to see her dad, she should be back shortly."

Iris turns to look at him as she takes her scarf and coat off handing them to Danny. She raises her eyebrows and asks.

"You let her go alone?"

Danny lying "She insisted" he hadn't really put up much of a fight when she left.

"Have you called her to see if she's OK?"

Danny feeling a little irritated at Iris' questioning "I'll call her now" he walks to the living room and picks up his mobile and calls Susan's mobile. The phone goes straight to voicemail "Damn it, she must have it off."

Iris playing devil's advocate "Or?"

"I'll call the restaurant" he dials the restaurant number that goes to voicemail also "Fuck! Fuck!" Danny's frustration is clear "Now I've got to..." before he can finish his sentence the land line rings. He rushes to the phone thinking it's probably Susan, maybe her battery went. He answers it "Hello."

The voice on phone has an Eastern European accent "Hello? Is Miss Chang there?"

"No, this is her partner can I help?"

Voice on phone "I hope so, my name is Clara, I work at the restaurant, there has been a terrible accident involving her parents, can you get hold of her?"

"I've been trying, she is supposed to be at the restaurant with her father now, are you telling me she is not there and what accident?"

Clara voice shows her distress "She is not here and her parents are... they're..." Clara sounds like she has been crying and is trying to hold it together "Mr and Mrs Chang are dead."

Iris has been listening to every word and she knew this conversation would not end with an "OK, great to hear from you. Take care."

"Have you called the police?"

"Yes."

"Are you alone?"

"No there are a couple of other waiters here."

"I'm coming there. If Susan shows up, get her to call me" he ends the call and looks at Iris "That was a waiter from the restaurant. Susan's parents are dead. A terrible accident apparently."

Iris nods slowly "Been a lot of those recently especially involving people we know. What happened?"

Danny is trying to call Susan again "Fuck! She's still going to voicemail. Her phone isn't even on. If she wasn't at the restaurant maybe she's OK."

Iris dubiously "Sure, Susan is probably sitting in a Costa somewhere working on her CV."

"You have to be such a bitch?"

"You do mean realist."

"I'm going to the restaurant "You are welcome to stay here or come."

Iris briefly ponders the irony that yet again she and Danny are in a hotel room. They have only ever had sex in hotel rooms and the odd spur of the moment public areas "I think I'll just wait here. What about the reporter? Want me to handle that?"

"No' I'll cancel her en-route" Danny coats up and grabs his keys from the hallway table. As he opens the door to leave he hears Iris shout.

"Where's the bar?"

Danny hurrying out points "Over there" and leaves.

Iris checks the contents of the bar, but nothing takes her fancy. She sees a wine list on the bar surface. As she reads the list of reds she notices a particular bottle she had had once when she and Danny started fucking around. A bottle of La Rioja Alta 904 Gran Reserva 1985.

"Nice" she whispers and picks up the phone to order room service.

Danny arrives at the restaurant in a black cab. There are two ambulances, three marked police cars and a small crowd gathered outside. As he approaches the restaurant a plain clothes female officer stops him "Sorry, closed."

Danny "My partner's parents own this place. I just want to make sure she's OK" Danny hears a familiar voice through the crowd.

"Let him through" It's DI Blaine.

Danny approaching DI Blaine "What happened? is Susan here?"

"We're not sure, and no, she isn't. Looks like some sort of accident with the oven" Danny remembers Iris' words "Mr and Mrs Chang were found dead in the large oven. Burnt to death."

"Jesus, Susan was supposed to be here. She's not answering her phone."

"When did you last see her?"

"About two hours ago."

"Hardly missing person territory yet. You sure she's not just gone somewhere to be alone?"

Danny gets closer to the policeman "Officer, seven people related to us are dead. Susan is supposed to be here right now, where you are clearing away her parents' dead bodies. Do you really think she's merrily sipping on a cuppa somewhere?"

"Where did you see her last?"

"At our hotel."

"Were you the last person to see her?"

"I don't fucking know. She must have gone past hotel reception and what the hell are you getting at?"

"I have to ask Mr Havers. Where were you for the past couple of hours?"

Danny shakes his head in disbelief "At the hotel, sitting and waiting alone for Susan to return for a meeting with a journalist."

"Journalist?"

"Yes, Susan, Iris and I are going to involve the media to help find David Todd since you don't believe the evidence points that way."

"Just a minute please" he dials a number on his mobile and turns to speak privately. He speaks in a quiet voice and ends the call "DI James will be out in a moment to talk to you. We got a flask with tea and coffee, want some?"

Danny senses the change in tone since mentioning the media "No thank you" he waits. As he waits he observes the crowd wondering if David might have hung around to revel in his handiwork.

Iris sips the wine. Mellow, rich, with a gentle after burn. Danny will have a shit fit when he sees this on his bill. As iris drinks the wine she feels a familiar urge. Iris has always enjoyed the company of men. Not for their wit or conversation, but purely for her entertainment. She enjoyed sex and was easily bored with just one partner. Danny was probably the longest sexual relationship she had ever had. Roger didn't count since he would rather stick his tongue into a chocolate éclair than her pussy and lost interest in sex about a year after they got married. Food was Roger's thing. Smear custard on his cock and if he could reach it with his mouth he would have been the happiest fucker alive. The urge to pick up a man, take him somewhere and just dominate him, make him do anything she wanted. The so called superior gender was indeed the stupider gender. She was lucky that they mostly think with the cells between their legs. She'd had men vowing to leave their wives after just one time with her. Why? Why would she want a weak, pathetic man who couldn't respect the vows he'd taken to be true to that one person? No, Iris was happy to use men as men have used women over the ages. She wasn't trying to get back at the stupider gender, she just enjoyed sex.

Iris looks at her watch and savours some more wine. It's going to be some time till Danny gets back and whilst there's a slim chance he may return with Susan, she sees no point in waiting for the happy couple to return; she may as well pop to a bar near the hotel and continue the drinking there. There are lots of young men desperately looking for a little fun at this time of year and she could do with a little fun. Iris picks up the phone and asks reception to order her a Taxi.

DI James emerges from the restaurant and heads to Danny and DI Blaine "What's all this about you talking to the media?" she's not happy.

Danny "What choice have you left us? You've made us suspects and are completely unwilling to pursue David. What do you think? This just another coincidence? Fuck no! It's David! He's out there."

James "Mr Havers, we can only follow the evidence and right now this scene shouts suicide. We found accounts ledgers which with even my limited finance knowledge points to this place being a loss maker. Big losses year after year. My guess is that they had enough and just decided to end it all. Some people just crack."

Danny flabbergasted by her stupidity "Is the oven electric or gas?"

"Electric, why?"

"Because what man chooses to crank up an electric oven and says to his wife "Come my dear, let's die an agonising and horrific death to find some peace. No, you slit each other's wrists or you put a gun in your mouth, but you do not roast your loved one in an electric oven to golden crispy fucking brown" Danny looks at James and Blaine to see if his point has been made "Now either you get the media involved or I'll do it and make fucking sure they know the Police knew there is a serial killer out there and you've done fuck all about it."

The two DIs look at each other and step aside for a quite confab. They return.

Blaine "OK Mr Havers we will arrange a press conference here and now. Do you have a recent picture of Susan?"

"Yes, on my phone. I've got loads."

James "An officer will come over to select one shortly."

James and Blaine leave and head to an unmarked police car. They get in and make a call they know will upset their superior.

Danny phones Susan again, still no answer. He calls Iris; she picks up "Hello."

Danny "Iris, good news, the Police are about to hold a press conference to spotlight David. I think you should come."

Iris mockingly "Great news, but pass. I'm going to have a little fun and head back to the hotel for hopefully a shit load more fun."

Danny gets her drift "No Iris, it's too risky. Come here by Taxi or stay in the hotel."

"Too late, I'm here now. I'll be fine. You just focus on finding Susan" she ends the call.

Danny frustrated by Iris' attitude or just a little jealous of whoever is about to get lucky "Shit! Fucking idiot is going to get herself killed."

He knows his best bet of stopping David is to ensure the press conference goes ahead. If he leaves the scene now James and Blaine may well have a change of heart. The plain clothes officer who stopped him earlier approaches asking to see the photos of Susan.

Iris enters the Raven Lounge, an establishment for people who would rather the price of the drinks act as a filter to ensure only a discerning clientele frequented the establishment. This made them feel privileged and safe. It was also a good place to network, make deals and hook-up. A waiter approaches her to take her coat and scarf. He ushers her to a table; she declines the table and opts for a booth. The bar is dimly lit with a very modern look. Glass tables, with comfy designer chairs, nooks with sofas and secluded booths with even dimmer lighting for ultimate privacy.

Iris takes a seat in a booth with the bar to her left. She orders a Grey Goose and blood orange. Having surveyed the occupants of the bar on the way in, she is disappointed with the place. Four tables with parties of three or four, a couple with couples and two single men at the bar; both hideous. Her drink arrives and she takes a sip testing the strength. This place only serves a minimum of double. The mix is perfect. Iris finishes the drink quickly, raises her hand and another is en-route.

Three drinks later and Iris is ready to leave and move on to different hunting ground. As she drains the last bit of blood orange vodka mix from the third drink she hears a man say.

"Can I say you are the most desirable woman I've seen since my year six art teacher."

"If you're looking for an art teacher you'd better move on" she looks at her admirer. Wow, young, about twenty five, six feet tall and bloody good looking in a Sean Connery rugged kind of way. A bit of stubble on a strong chin. Suited and booted definitely a product of the City.

Admirer "Hi, I'm still an art lover but that's not what I'm after tonight. My name is Duncan, can I join you?"

"Please. Sit." Duncan sits opposite Iris and raises his arm. A waiter moves into action knowing exactly what each patron wants to drink.

Duncan "I saw you come in and assumed a woman as beautiful as you would be shortly followed by a very apologetic partner."

"Well I guess you figured wrong. These days my partners are dropping like flies. Now enough of the flattery just tell me what you have in mind" she just wants to hear him say "Take you out of here, tear your clothes off, lick your pussy and fuck you hard till you cum" he doesn't disappoint. They order their bills, pay and leave together.

Iris has had the better part of a bottle of wine and three double Vodkas. She's feeling it. They walk about one hundred meters to Duncan's car and he helps her in. They drive in silence at first then Iris asks.

"Where are we going? How about my place?"

"I thought we could go to mine."

Iris' head is swirling "OK, yours it is."

After what seems a very short drive the car comes to a halt. Duncan opens the door helping her out. Still feeling the drink Iris follows Duncan into an alleyway. He opens a door and ushers her in. It's dark but he flicks a light on. It's weird, the light is red. The room is illuminated in red light and there is a bed in the middle, a sink with a mirror above it in a corner and a solitary cosy chair in another. Iris' booze soaked mind assumes he's just a little fucked up. Good looking, but fucked up. Her type.

Duncan "Strip" his voice has changed. He's more commanding. As if she has no choice in the matter. Duncan takes a seat on the bed. He watches as Iris starts to strip. Inebriated, she manages to strip down to her panties and bra.

Duncan "All of it."

Iris removes the remaining garments. Duncan gets up and takes his shirt off followed by his shoes, trousers and underwear. He's erect and ready for action. This is what she wanted. The seedy setting, the stranger, she is excited. Duncan comes close to her. She expects him to kiss her, but he just says.

"On your knees" she obeys. She is face to cock. It's a nice cock, not huge, about the right diameter and just right for a few hours of fucking. Iris had extensive experience sizing up cocks. Duncan reaches behind her head and grabs her hair from the back with his left hand. He pulls her hair back lifting her head up so he can look into her eyes. With his right hand he takes his stiff cock and slaps her repeatedly on the left side of her face with it.

"Ready bitch" he rubs his cock on her cheek as if caressing her face. Then he positions the end of his cock on her lips. Iris opens her mouth and licks the head slowly. As she instinctively starts to work Duncan's penis she realises her usual control over the man is missing. Usually it's her in the driving seat, ordering her eager bitch to do her bidding. She wants to reverse the roles currently being played out. She pulls away from his cock and tries to stand. He's not having any of it. He yanks down on her hair keeping her on her knees. He starts to pump his cock in and out of her mouth. She feels him trying to go deep. He's getting rougher and starting to talk shit.

"Take it all you little slut. You're mine tonight" he suddenly lets go of her hair and pulls his cock out "Get on the bed he orders" Iris wants to say "No" but can't. She gets on the bed and lies on her back "Spread your legs" she complies still not understanding how this man is in control.   By now she'd have him going down on her, pleasuring her, but here she is legs spread with him about to mount her. He climbs on top of her grinning with anticipation. She wants to spin him over, get on top and fuck him. She so desperately wants to be in control. He positions his cock at the entrance of her vagina rubbing the head up and down her slit testing to ensure she is wet. She is. He pushes into her, his cock slides in easily.

"Your pussy is so fucking hot and wet slut" he pulls out slightly and pushes again. Iris arches her hips upward to meet his thrust. He enters her fully. She moans as he fills her pussy. She moans more as he slowly slides his cock out then quickly in and grinds his cervix against her clit. She is enjoying this, but it's still not what she wants. She pushes with her right leg to turn them both over, but he's resists grabbing both her wrists and placing her arms above her head pinning them. He starts to pound her harder and faster. She's pinned, helpless and completely in his control. Unable to do anything else she gives in to this man. She feels the power he has over her and somehow it excites her now. She feels his hard bulging cock being angrily rammed in and out of her and she likes it. Her breathing quickens as she feels her orgasm starting to build. She can tell from his facial expressions he's not far off. As he thrusts into her she meets him by lifting her hips. Then she feels it.

One more thrust and "Oh God! Oh fucking God" she cums hard, soaking his cock and balls.

As she cums he continues to fuck her hard. Then he starts to make "I'm about to cum noises" he lets her wrists go, pushes her legs over his shoulder and leans forward to pin her wrists over her head again. He really goes for it now. Using the bounce from the bed he speeds up the rate of fucking like a man possessed. As he pumps his cock into her overflowing pussy their bodies make a moist slapping sound each time they meet; like some weird sexual metronome .

Iris orgasms again "Fuck! Oh fuck!"

She looks at this beautiful, crazy man pumping away and about to cum in her. Something she never lets any man do without a condom, but right now she doesn't give a damn. As she watches him heading to his final destination something suddenly doesn't look right. The man she started fucking was young with dark hair and a firm and fairly muscular body. Now he looks older, much older with grey hair, stubble and the body of a fifty year old. It hits her. The man fucking her is David. Still pinned she tries to push him away with her legs but she can't. Her legs just rest on his shoulders as he fucks her.

Iris breathing hard and shaking her head from side to side sees David's grinning face "Get off you fuck!" she shouts. He slows down feeling himself about to cum.

David sweating and still grinning "I'm going to cum in your pussy slut then we're going to have some more fun."

He speeds up the pace again then it happens. As his cock convulses squirting into her he looks into her eyes,

"Wow that was intense" he keeps her pinned waiting for the sensations to subside. Iris is confused. How can this be? Had she drunk that much? David slides out his softening dick.

Iris is disgusted "You fucking animal, this is rape" she tries to move off the bed, but it's like she's been tied down.

David walks to a sink in the corner of the room "It's only rape if you were unwilling."

"You drugged me you fucking piece of shit."

"I assure you I most certainly did not drug you. You saw what you wanted and you took what you wanted."

"Why can't I get up? Where am I?"

David washes his hands and takes a wet flannel to his genitals. He throws the flannel into a bin liner next to the sink.

"Ah, good questions. It took me a while to find this place. Upstairs used to be a strip club and down here is where if you wanted a little more that titilation and were willing to pay all the goodies on offer were at your disposal."

Iris still struggling "let me go you bastard."

"That's not down to me and to be honest I wouldn't know how to" he looks at her lying there helpless.

Time to crank up the mood a little "Well, now we've reacquainted ourselves let me introduce our audience tonight. Come in please gentlemen" as David utters the words four men of varying ages enter the room through the door. They are naked. The men all have a glazed look in their eyes as if drugged or hypnotised or something. They approach the bed two on each side of her. It's too dark to get a good look at them "These horny assholes have been watching us through that darkened wall. It's really darkened glass. This room used to host live sex shows and men would watch from behind the glass while they wanked and as you can see they are well and truly in the mood."

Iris in abject fear "No David, please. We were friends; please don't let them do this to me. Please" she pleads.

David shakes his head "Why does everyone keep playing the friend card. Do you people suddenly forget what you did to me when it suits you?"

"Please David; I'll do anything, just stop this."

"Come on Iris, your sexual appetite is legendary. You fucked most of the young men in the building, and there are eleven floors! You can surely handle four out of shape, haven't had a fuck in a long time homeless men. Don't worry, I made sure they wiped their icky bits" David walks to another corner of the room and sits in a cosy chair carefully placed to observe the action.

Iris can smell these men. They smell of perspiration, stale piss and a hint of shit. They can't have bathed in months. She is grateful for the poor lighting. God knows what they look like.

David gives the command "Do it!"

They men climb onto the bed on their knees and get close enough to her so the smell is strong enough to make her gag. As they get close two either side of her she see sees they are fully erect. They take their penises in their hands and start to masturbate. Something in Iris stirs, that longing to be in control coming back. These men are turned on by her. Just looking at her naked body is enough to make them want to take matters into their own hands. Suddenly she finds herself saying.

"Do it. Cum on my face."

With that encouragement the men reposition themselves to get a good shot at Iris' face. "

Come on, let me feel that hot cum on my face you useless piece of shit" the words are uttered by her but it's not her. She hears them start to groan. They wank furiously. As she holds out her tongue it's too much for the wanker closest to her head on her left. He shoots; it hits her on the forehead and down the left cheek. Something is wrong, Iris expected it to be warm, but this is hot. She feels a sharp pain where the cum hit. She wants to wipe it off, but can't move her arms. It sizzles slightly like acid burning her face. Another wanker offloads, this time on the right. Again a burning sensation "Stop! Stop!! She screams, but they keep at it. That last one was a lot; it hit the right side of her face, her nose and was dripping down to her ear. Burning with the same fizzing sound as it travels. Iris is screaming, but the men are oblivious. Then another pops. This was the mother load. Covering her nose, mouth and chin she spits and tries to blow away the caustic liquid. Finally the last one groans and delivers. Her face is covered and burning. She thrashes from side to side trying to get it off. The men hear David's voice say something and slip off the bed. They retreat to their observation point in the voyeur room. Iris is trashing about screaming in agony.

David "There is a sink in the corner Iris. Wash you face" she can move, she leaps off the bed and stumbles to the sink. She runs the water quickly splashing it on her face wiping away the sticky mess. She washes till the burning stops. As her breathing slows she glimpses the bottom of a mirror above the sink at about head height. She rises to look at herself. She lets out a soul destroying scream followed by.

"You fucking bastard! What have you done to me!" her face is beyond recognition. It's as if she dipped her face in a bowl of acid. Red, raw and burnt.

"Maybe you're like a caterpillar. Underneath all that ugliness is a butterfly waiting to come out".

As his words finish Iris peers closer into the mirror. She reaches for a loose piece of seared skin on her forehead with her right hand and tugs at it. It comes loose revealing a two centimetre length of what looks like smooth flawless skin. Amazed she feels for another piece of damaged skin and peels that off too. More beautiful flawless skin. She continues peeling, feeling happier and happier as she reveals skin like which she had when she was eighteen.

Finally finished she turns to David "Look David, I'm beautiful."

"You look like shit to me, but beauty is in the eye of the beholder" confused Iris turns to the mirror again screams and faints. She had been peeling her skin off all the time.

12 Invidia

About the same time as Iris was arriving at the Raven Lounge, a television crew for the BBC was arriving at the Jade Dragon Restaurant. The Police had already asked Danny to make himself scarce during the interview which would be handled by DI James. Danny sits in an unmarked police car still trying to get hold of Susan. He knows she is in trouble, but is helpless to do anything. He tries Iris, no answer, but he suspects she has found a young victim and is probably busy feeding her desires.

Danny watches as James and Blaine speak to the reporter. A young mixed race man about twenty eight, very slim build and well groomed. The police had decided to give the information relating to the incident at the restaurant and the deaths of his other colleagues to the media without them appearing before the camera.

As they talk to the BBC reporter other reporters gather round as details of numerous deaths are revealed. The pack smells blood. This was breaking news with front page newspaper splash written all over it. Danny can see the media pack getting more and more excited. If it wasn't his life involved he'd probably be glued to the television when it is reported. Danny delighted in other people's misery. He envied their successes and relished their misfortunes. He wondered how David is feeling now seeing the man who sent him to the gutter falling in the same way. The pack is getting animated, shoving microphones in the faces of the officer. Danny knows this is big and big means National coverage. David will have nowhere to hide. That fucker should be in custody by morning. He watches as the police excuse themselves from the pack. The pack scatters to get the news out there.

Danny exits the car and heads to James and Blaine. He brushes past a couple of uniformed officers and taps James on the shoulder "When will they air?" he asks.

James "Any minute now. Looks like they're going with a probable serial killer in the City of London. Sound familiar?"

Blaine "They have Susan's picture and we've provided some details of the deaths along with Todd's last DVLA photo. I suggest you go home and lock the doors Mr Havers. If Susan returns or gets in touch please let us know. What about Mrs Caldwell. Any idea where she is?"

Danny shrugs his shoulders "She was at the hotel, but left to... well to have a drink I think" can't really say she's gone cock hunting. Not a few days after the death of her husband. Danny turns to see several television crews hurriedly setting up to air the good news. He decides the police are right and home is the best place he can be now. He sets off to find a black cab.

He walks a couple of blocks and as he turns the corner he bumps into a man rushing from the opposite direction.

The man "Shit sorry mate, just a bit late for a date."

The man checks the time on his watch. Danny glances at the man's watch. A Rolex Submariner Date, white gold solid link oyster bracelet with the blue dial.

Danny "No problem" he wants the watch, not one like it, but that watch. He shakes the thought from his head then proceeds to follow the man as Mr late for a date rushes off.

Danny thinks to himself "What the fuck am I doing?" but still he keeps following the man. He needs to have that watch, to feel it on his wrist, to look at it and know it's his. He has wanted that watch all his life, from ever since he can remember that watch has been his goal. He has to have it "Why am I having a fucking Gollum moment now? Just stop and go home!" he tries hard to resist the pull of the wrist piece, but onward he rushes. He is within ten feet of the man who is now becoming aware of Danny's presence behind him. The man turns to see Danny approaching quickly.

Man "What mate? Did you lose something? Danny gets to the man and grabs at his left wrist trying to unclasp the watch "What the fuck! Mate you better let go or I'm gonna fucking knock you out." The man is big, a couple of inches taller than Danny and broad with it. Like some sort of off duty bouncer. He pushes Danny back. Danny comes at him again and the man reacts; violently. He swings a massive right to Danny's face and it connects knocking the desire for the watch out of his mind. Danny reels back and lands on his arse.

The man shouts "If I weren't late I'd stay and fuck you up."

With that her resumes his journey. A couple of tourists try to help Danny up. He shakes off their help and gets up on his own. The pain in his face coming on now. Danny lurches to the kerb side and hails a black cab.

The cab journey is done in silence. The driver senses something is wrong and just listens to the radio. LBC is on and reports of the killings and missing person are featured. Danny's phone whistles indicating he has received a text. He quickly gets the phone from his coat pocket and checks it.

"Thank God" he says to himself. It's Susan. Her text says she went back to the flat after seeing her parents to pick up a few more things and fell asleep. She wants him to meet her there. Danny is relieved. At last one of them has not fallen victim to that arsehole. He gives the taxi driver his apartment address and they set off. He knows he should call the police, but he just wants to make sure Susan is well and maybe have that conversation about what can and can't be mentioned before the media get to her.

The taxi arrives at his apartment block; he pays and heads to the lobby. The night Concierge Gary is on duty "Evening Gary" Danny tries to hide the left side of his face where Mr late for a date knocked some sense into him.

"Evening Mr Havers, everything OK? I saw the news and couldn't believe it"

"Yes, just in a bit of a rush. Anyone asking after me or any visitors?"

"No Sir, been quiet. Just a couple of residents and the maintenance guy. Something to do with the electrics, so expect them to play up a little till he's finished. Any problems please call me."

"What time did Miss Chang get here?"

"I only came on duty an hour ago. Ronin was on before that."

Danny "OK, I'll see you in the morning. Good night."

Danny takes the lift to his floor. He thinks how good it would be to open the door and find Susan lying on the sofa having a snooze as he has often done in the past. He opens the door and enters. It's dark. The auto sensors on the lights usually switch on the hallway lights as soon as the door is opened. Is this what Gary was talking about? He is wary and gets his phone out to use the torch app. There is a lamp on the hallway table which he aims for, he tries the lamp and it works. The light is dim but better than darkness. He looks for the intercom phone to call Gary to find out exactly what the maintenance guy is doing, but it's not in the holder. He walks slowly to the living room still uneasy; he opens the door again expecting the auto light to come on. It does, but very dimly. He peers into the poorly lit room cursing the maintenance guy. He heads to the coffee table in the middle of the room then hears a sound. A whispered voice.

"Help me" Danny responds to the direction of the sound.

The living area adjoins the dining area which has a small glass dining table with four chairs. As his eyes become accustomed to the dim light he sees Susan sitting motionless on one of the dining chairs. Her head bowed and, her hands on her lap.

"Susan! Thank God!" he rushes to her "Are you OK?" as he gets to her he sees she is holding a meat cleaver in her right hand. He stops, his mind on high alert now "Susan, what are you doing with that. You don't have to worry; David can't get to you in here. You're safe. Let me have the cleaver.

Susan emotionless "No."

Danny is about to try to reason further when he hears a muffled groan behind him. He spins around and sees a woman sitting on another dining chair in a similar position as Susan, but this woman has a blood soaked pillow case on her head. Danny recognises the clothing.

"Iris, Oh my god Iris, what happened" Possibilities rush through his mind. Maybe Susan found out about him and Iris and, well she's holding a meat cleaver. Danny's interest in Iris' welfare is quickly overtaken by his own self interest "Susan, please I can explain" Iris whimpers and Susan remains silent retreating to her safe place as Danny finds the words to explain away his infidelity.

"Susan I swear it was just... "before he can finish the words Danny hears the voice that explains it all.

"Hello old friend" Its David.

Danny sees David standing behind another dining chair smiling "Hello Danny, miss me?"

Danny reaches for his phone in his trouser pocket as he responds to David "The police are looking for you. In fact they are on their way" he bluffs as he feels for the phone.

David "Stop!" Danny has the phone in his hand but stops as David orders "Come take a seat, I think the four of us have a few things to work out. Danny against his will moves toward David. He stands opposite him eye to eye. David holds his stare "Sit you piece of shit."

The three chairs are arranged in a triangle so each occupant can see the others. David moves to the centre of the triangle excited by what is about to come.

"This is corny, but this IS a love triangle" David wants to savour every moment "Danny, I believe you were in confession mode. Do you want to get it all off your chest?"

Danny scared, but wanting to sound defiant "Fuck you, the police are will be here any minute. The Concierge will have seen you coming in. You're fucked you psychopath."

"Have you ever noticed how maintenance people seem to go unnoticed? Even better when the building wants to make sure they are not seen by residents so they install a maintenance lift."

Danny still bluffing "The police are sending a protection team. You better go while you still can." "Please go" Danny pleads in his head "Please, please just go."

"Back to your confession. Perhaps Iris would like to see what's going on" David walks to Iris' chair and stands behind her "Dunnah!" he whips off the pillow case.

Danny "Oh my god! Oh my god! What the fuck!" Iris face is gone, replaced by a bloody mess of skinless tissue and bones.

Danny panics, starting to hyperventilate. The mother of all anxiety attacks. No reaction from Susan. She has found somewhere safe. She's ten and just got home from school. Her mum has given her a snack and she settles down for her weekly fix of Scooby Doo. The theme music plays. She is content.

Danny "What... What the fuck. You killed her!"

David "No, she's alive. I needed her for the "love triangle" gag" David grins looking at Danny "Iris please say hello to Danny" Iris obeys, she lifts her head and looks directly at Danny. Danny looks away unable to see anything of Iris in this creature. David whispers in Iris' ear and she speaks to Danny.

"Hey Babe, how about a blow job?" she stands slowly and does a walking dead towards Danny who musters all his strength trying to get up, pushing hard with his legs, but he can't. He wants to tip the chair over but can't. Iris shuffles ever closer.

David "Wow Danny, you are a lucky man. All these women wanting a piece of your dick."

Iris stands in front of Danny, blood dripping from her chin. She kneels in front of him. As he gets a close up of her he starts to shake with fear. She reaches for his belt and slowly undoes it.

Danny desperately searches for a way to stop the scene being played out "Please, I've got forty million in two offshore accounts; more in stocks. You can have it all. Please stop this!"

"I know you have, you seem to think money can buy you anything; even forgiveness. You were my best friend. I trusted you and you fucked me and my family. This is not my doing. It's yours!"

Iris unbuttons Danny's trouser and pulls the fly zip down dripping blood onto his lap. She pulls at his boxer shorts to get to his penis.

David comes in for a closer look "You've always wanted what the other person had, wanted what you couldn't have, and never satisfied with what you had."

Danny a little annoyed at David's analysis mostly because it's true "Fuck you David, you always wanted more, you accumulated far more than we did, but you never shared that wealth proportionately. You kept most of it to yourself."

"Yes I did, but it was my ideas and hard work that kept the deals coming. I was responsible for setting up and closing deals and if it went wrong the buck stopped with me; but you know that."

Iris fumbles at Danny's shorts trying to locate little Danny who seems to have beat a very hasty retreat.

Danny "We can start again, we have money, you still have it in you, we can start again."

"National manhunt for a serial killer, my face all over the news. Think I'll pass. How about we play a little game of retribution, but first I think Iris is felling a little frisky."

Iris locates little Danny and pulls him out. He is decidedly not in the mood. Iris encourages him with a little masturbation then she dips her head opening her mouth. Her lips are gone exposing her upper and lower teeth. Danny freaks out desperately trying to writhe away. Blood dripping on little Danny. Her teeth reach him and she opens wider and slops floppy Little Danny into her mouth. Iris works little Danny with her tongue and teeth. Blood now all over little Danny. Danny can't look. He closes his eyes then he feels Iris' teeth start to bite a little on his dick.

"Fuck that hurts, stop" she keeps going, biting a little harder "Stop! Stop! That's too fucking hard" she continues, her upper and lower incisors clenching together. Danny screams as she draws blood and continues to grind her teeth cutting away at the sinews of his penis, then she pulls back, Danny in excruciating pain opens his eyes to see Iris staring at him, his cock in her mouth. His mind can't process this. His fucking dick is gone. Iris chews as if chomping on a chewy Lion chocolate bar. Danny still screaming wants to faint but hears David's voice.

"Susan, are you going to let her do that to your man in front of you. With that comment Susan leaps out of her chair and sprints to Iris. Susan is still in her safe place. The theme song plays.

"Scooby Dooby Doo, where are you; we've got some work to do now" she is behind Iris.

She raises the cleaver high above her head to get a good downward swing.

"Scooby Dooby Doo, where are you, we need some help from you now."

She brings the cleaver down with all her strength.

"Come on Scooby Doo, I see you pretending you've got a sliver."

The cleaver hits Iris' head dead centre. The cleaver slices into her head to about halfway. It gets stuck, Iris' body slumps forward into Danny's lap. Susan pulls at the cleaver to free it.

"But you're not fooling me, cause I see the way you shake and shiver."

She frees the cleaver and raises it again; before she can strike again David shouts "Enough!" she puts her hands to her side still holding the cleaver, dips her head and walks back to her chair.

"You know we've got a mystery to solve so Scooby Doo be ready for your act, Don't hold back!" she resumes her position in the chair.

David takes a good look at Iris to make sure she's is dead. He pulls her off Danny's lap. What's left of little Danny is squirting blood "Looks like she really did want a piece of your dick. Now let's address this thing you have about what you see is what you want. Seems to me that we should work on this particular personality flaw. Don't you agree?"

Danny catches on quickly and starts begging again "Please David, Please, I've suffered enough. Please."

"OK, how about we play a game? Susan, get the paring knife please" Susan gets up and goes to the kitchen "I have to compliment you on a very well equipped kitchen Danny. Everything needed for a killing spree" Susan returns with the paring knife in her left hand and the bloodied cleaver in the other. By some unheard command she kicks Iris' body aside and kneels before Danny. She puts the knife in Danny's right hand. He immediately tries to lunge at David, but can't.

David "Your choice Danny, stick that knife in your eye or hers."

Danny holds the knife, armed, unable to use it against David. "Hurry Danny, you're cock is still bleeding, Can't keep that up for long. Your eye or hers now!"

Danny knows it's going to be Susan's eye. He tries to rationalise it. She has clearly had some sort of mental break. Probably won't even feel it. With no hesitation he raises the knife and is about to shove it into Susan's left eye when David says.

"Susan he's picked you" she stands up fast dropping the cleaver and grabbing Danny's hand. The theme song to Scooby Doo is on repeat.

"Scooby Dooby Doo where are you, we've got some work to do now" Susan takes the knife and straddles Danny sitting on his bleeding cock stump.

Danny "No! No!" She pulls his head back by his hair using her left hand giving her a good look at his eyes. Her face expressionless she brings the knife tip to within a centimetre of his left pupil. Danny begs again and again as Susan moves the knife millimetre by millimetre closer.

"Scooby Dooby Doo where are you we need some help from you now."

The ultra sharp knife tip makes contact with the green of his eye. A little scratch at first then searing pain as the paring knife continues its steady course into the pupil to the centre of the eyeball. Susan is steady as a rock blissfully unaware of the pain she is causing.

"Come on Scooby Doo I see you pretending you've got a sliver."

Danny's body convulses as his eyeball oozes fluid down his cheek. His right eye shut from the pain he doesn't even hear David instruct Susan to stop. She pulls the knife out slowly. Susan remains straddled on Danny.

Danny's head slumps forward desperate to faint, to pass out.

"Just fucking kill me please, just kill me."

David "Too easy, too quick and we still have to address another of your flaws. The lying" Danny knows where this is going. Why can't he just pass out?

"They're going to find you and fucking lock you up for the rest of your life you cunt."

"I don't think so. Even the police were dubious about my involvement in the other deaths. In fact, fingers pointed to you. Over there on the coffee table are photos taken of you and Iris having an afternoon off? In here we have the evidence of a fatal love triangle. Susan finds out you've been playing away, the three of you meet up and here we are. All the time she was missing she was waiting here for you and Iris. That reminds me" David goes to a corner of the room and picks up a black bin liner. He goes to the chair where Iris was sitting and empties the contents onto the floor around the chair "Iris' face or skin, you know what I mean" the faintest hint of a smile seems to flash across Susan's face for a moment.

David gets back to business "About this rather disturbing trait of yours. Open your mouth and stick your tongue out" Danny tries desperately to defy but he opens his mouth and sticks his tongue out. David moves in for a close up "Now Susan" she holds his tongue with her left hand. It's strangely dry and coarse to the touch. She places the knife to the right of Danny's tongue. He gargles something then.

"You know we've got a mystery to solve so Scooby Doo be ready for your act, don't hold back."

A swift swipe across the tongue and it comes away clean. Blood spurts onto her face. She jumps off his lap letting go of the tongue and stands watching as he bleeds from his groin, eye and mouth. Another unspoken command and she places the knife in Danny's right hand with the blade point facing up; she steadies it on his right knee. Susan drops to her knee, the knife enters upward under her chin, through her mouth cavity and into her skull. Susan's body falls back onto the floor. Danny makes glugging noises as his blood chokes him. David watches Danny as his body convulses processing the shock and the pain. He looks into Danny's remaining eye as his heart shuts down. The eye remains open staring back at David.

13 Avaritia

David arrives at the lair. He is elated and can't wait to see his new best buddy. He races to the bedroom reaches under the bed and pulls the shoebox out looking at Shithead.

David smiles "It's done. Both your arms are gone. They're all dead. I can get my life back again."

David didn't get any food or booze on his way home. He didn't want to be recognised. He was a National celebrity now. Name and face all over the television and by morning in all the papers. He had stocked up previously on Shithead's favourite beer and had some left over KFC from lunch.

Shithead was oddly silent "What? Nothing to say?"

Shithead "Hungry."

David gives it what it wants. It falls asleep so does David.

In a small shared two bedroom flat above the Sunshine Diner the delivery driver who had been pranked a few weeks before is on his mobile to the police "Look, I can't be certain cos this guy had a beard, but kind of looked like the man you're after. I remember it cos I had to give the food away free" he listens for a moment while the person on the other end talks "No please, not on hold again. Fuck it" he ends the call intending to call later when it's not so busy.

David's favourite shop, Saleem is on the phone while serving impatient customers "Yes, I want to report that I seen that crazy man from the telly. He shop here all the time. I got CCTV from yesterday. When you're coming? Later? What time? He could come in and any minute now. OK. I'm open till twelve" he ends the call.

David wakes to the sound of Shithead in his head "Hungry."

David "OK I'll get us some breakfast, but I'm going to have to cover up. Shithead speaks to Danny.

Danny "What now? They're all dead and you're still here. Are you real or just in my head?" he asks not really expecting an answer; just the usual cryptic crap. Shithead hisses, this time not in his head. He moves closer to the box to hear.

"What? What was that?"

Shithead whispers "One more."

"One more what? One more drink?"

"One more must die."

David pulls back "You said six; six and then some are dead. It's over."

"One more must die."

David had been happy. He just had to find a way to make sure none of the killings led directly back to him. He had worn gloves at all the scenes and then disposed of the gloves by burning them to be safe. He hadn't touched any of the bodies with the exception of Iris who against his will he fucked and left a lot of DNA in. Still with her promiscuous past it was believable they met up and one thing led to another.

"No you came to help me get revenge on them. It's over."

Shithead pauses then says "Not you."

David puzzled "What do you mean, not me?"

"Do you see any similarity between your friends and you?"

"Yeah, we all worked in the same field; banking."

"Do you see that you all share one particular character flaw?"

David is puzzled. He can't see where Shithead is going with this plus its voice is oddly calm "What? You going to preach to me about greed? Yes, I was, am greedy for success, who isn't?"

"They were willing to see you destroyed because of their greed. You were happy to watch them suffer for taking away what your greed had enabled you to accumulate. You are all the same."

"If you are so fucking judgemental why the hell did you help me kill them all?"

Shithead seems to smile "Firstly, I had no choice and secondly, it wasn't for you, it was for her."

David still puzzled "Her who?"

"Mary."

At the mention of her name a veil seems to lift from David's eyes. He suddenly feels weak and out of breath. He staggers back a little stumbling on something. He looks down to see what it is. His lovely clean basement flat doesn't look so clean now. Bottles are everywhere; empty booze bottles. Jack, Smirnoff, Courvoisier, empty bottles everywhere. All the time he thought he was sobering up, but Shithead blinded him. How could he drink that much and still be alive. Three weeks, must be at least three weeks since the winning ticket. He looks at his shaking hands and walks to the small mirror in the bathroom. He looks at his reflection. A living corpse, that's the only description of what looks back at him. David feels pain in his stomach and chest. He staggers back into the bedroom reaching for his phone. He holds the phone with both hands trying to dial 999. He reaches the bedroom breathless.

"What the fuck are you?" he fumbles with the phone accidently activating the camera. The pain in his chest grabs his attention fully. He lurches forward towards the shoebox pressing on the phone screen as he falls. He wants to smash the creature with his body as he impacts the floor, but he falls short of the shoebox. As the pain tightens in his chest and his eyes close he hears Shithead's unmistakable laugh.

"Heh, heh, heh."

A loud banging on the door of the basement flat "Police, open the door Mr Todd. We have a warrant."

No answer, they bang the door again a couple of times then decide to force entry. The door gives easily and several uniformed and plain clothes officers rush in. The first two in are armed with hand guns. The police quickly and carefully sweep the flat.

"In here!" one shouts "body on the floor!"

Two plain clothes officers carefully approach David's body prodding it with their shoes "Jesus one exclaims, he stinks. I think it's him."

Twenty minutes later the area on the street around the flat is cordoned off and forensics are on the scene. One of the Forensics officers is examining the body and finds something odd.

"Look at this. Some sort of worm or maggot coming out of his ear. The body hasn't been dead long enough for that" she tweezers the worm and bags it.

David died clinging to his mobile. Another officer carefully extracts the phone from his hand and looks at it. She notices the camera was activated and goes to the pictures. The only footage is a five second video. She plays it.

"Weird" she turns to her colleague "What do you make of this" she plays the video again. The video is taken by David before his death while trying to call 999 and as he fall towards the shoebox "See that some sort of doll in a box."

Other officer "Yeah what's so weird?"

Bemused officer "The box is over there, so where is the doll?"

8 am Saturday morning a week into December and an hour after David's body was found. Mary is awake heading downstairs to make herself a tea. She didn't get much sleep

with all that had been going on. She still had visions of Draper's eyes staring helplessly at her seemingly begging for help. She wasn't sure, but somehow she knew David was behind it all. It was that look he used to have when he had the upper hand in a deal and didn't want anyone else to know, but would send her a slight signal as if to say "It's OK. I'm in control here. She moves from the tiny kitchen to the living room. The boys will sleep till she wakes them. She's happy for them to sleep; gives her a bit of peace and quiet. She purposely doesn't put the television on. All those programs about Christmas and the adverts just reminds her of how tightly budgeted she is.

She had considered getting a payday loan, but dismissed the idea when she saw a money program with desperate people who had taken such loans become even more desperate after. She sits on the sofa and picks up her laptop from the coffee table. Time to check how far into her overdraft she was. She knew she would get paid early this month, but if she wasn't careful they'd have to live on water and air till end of January. She had to be strong and deny the kids any expensive gifts. By her calculations she should be six hundred and twenty pounds overdrawn. She has a limit of eight hundred. She clicks the NatWest icon and enters her PIN, fearing that her estimate may be wrong. Her account home page flashes up. Her eyes widen; Account balance £79,999,380.20 in credit. She blinks again to be sure, peering at the screen, then shouts.

"Kids! Get dressed! We're going shopping!"

The End?

Made in the USA
Columbia, SC
22 December 2018